Noah stood in the doorway, naked except for a towel slung carelessly around his hips.

He affected her in a way that was beyond her control. With him less than two feet away, she couldn't think. He shifted that dark, hypnotic gaze from her to his bed and back. Heat exploded inside her, sending stream after stream of hot, urgent sensations through her body. She trembled; her heart rate would not slow, her rapid intake of breath belied her composure.

He moved in her direction. 'My private space is off-limits.'

He was too gorgeous…too splendid to ignore. Whatever had happened to him five years ago, there was no outward indication that he was anything other than perfect. Even in the low light it was impossible to miss the sexual hunger glittering behind those deep brown eyes. His tone was thick with desire and promise, soft in a way that was lethal to all that made her a woman. 'I don't think you realise just how dangerous it is here for you…'

D0530524

Available in January 2004 from Silhouette Intrigue

Guardian of the Night

DEBRA WEBB

SILHOUETTE®
INTRIGUE™

*Silhouette and Colophon are registered trademarks of
Harlequin Books S.A., used under licence.*

First published in Great Britain 2004
Silhouette Books, Eton House, 18-24 Paradise Road,
Richmond, Surrey TW9 1SR

© Debra Webb 2003

ISBN 0 373 22701 9

46-0104

Printed and bound in Spain
by Litografia Rosés S.A., Barcelona

DEBRA WEBB

was born in Scottsboro, Alabama, USA, to parents who taught her that anything is possible if you want it badly enough. She began writing at age nine. Eventually, she met and married the man of her dreams, and tried some other occupations, including selling hoovers, working in a factory, a day-care centre, a hospital and a department store. When her husband joined the military, they moved to Berlin, Germany, and Debra became a secretary in the commanding general's office. By 1985, they were back in the States, and finally moved to Tennessee, to a small town where everyone knows everyone else. With the support of her husband and two beautiful daughters, Debra took up writing again, looking to mystery and films for inspiration. In 1998, her dream of writing for Silhouette came true. You can write to Debra with your comments at PO Box 64, Huntland, Tennessee 37345, USA.

Debra Webb on...

Her ultimate romantic meal:
Pizza and a coke in front of a good movie.

Her all-time favourite romantic movie:
Runaway Bride

**Her all-time favourite romantic song
or composition:**
'When a Man Loves a Woman' by Michael Bolton

The most romantic gesture or gift she has received:
My husband brought roses to me at my first
book signing!

**How she keeps the romance alive in her
relationship:**
By looking for the good, rather than picking
out the bad.

Her tip to make her readers lives more romantic:
Always, always live today like it's your last.

The most romantic place she's ever travelled to:
Paris, France.

Things are not always as they seem. These words are especially true of those with special circumstances. Sometimes all we take the time to see is what's on the outside of a person, never looking deeper, never noticing who they really are. This book is dedicated to a very special person whose life changed mine so profoundly and at the same time so wonderfully that my journey was forever changed. To my daughter, Erica Webb Jeffrey. You are an inspiration to us all. Love, Mom.

Chapter One

Darkness.

His only escape from the prison he called home.

The deserted beach stretched out before him like a vast, uncharted universe. It moved like a shadowy serpent, ever undulating. Waves crashed, slid away, leaving a glittering residue on the sand that captured the sparse light of the cloud-veiled moon. While he stood perfectly still, the breeze whispered through the night, urging him to enjoy the freedom only the too-short hours after the gloaming and before the dawn could offer.

Noah Drake closed his eyes and inhaled deeply of the thick salt air. He burrowed his toes in the sand, smiled and imagined the infinite grains hot from the scorching sun, the heat baking his bare feet. He summoned the memory of how the sunlight felt on his face, warm, like a lover's kiss. With more slow, deep breaths, he persuaded himself to relax and he could almost feel the golden brilliance touching him, healing him as nothing else could.

He opened his eyes.

It was only a memory.

Noah would never know that invigorating sensation

again. This was as close as he would get. The moon peeked from amid the voluminous purple clouds making the sand appear whiter, the water bluer. All else was lost to him. For five endless years he had been sentenced to darkness. The cold, empty truth filled him with an all-consuming rage. Adrenaline surged through his veins, as hot as Hades must surely be and as insistent as the breaking surf that was now as much a part of him as his own heartbeat.

So he tugged on the running shoes that lay at his feet and he ran.

Along the beach then through the dense forest that forged right up to the sand like a battalion of troops ready to conquer. Dense undergrowth closed in around him, and towering trees laden with moss rendered the shadows beneath impenetrable. All traces of the moon disappeared, all that remained was the silent foreboding. But that didn't stop Noah. His vision had long ago adjusted to this nocturnal existence, as his hearing had grown keener with the silence of his self-imposed exile from the human race.

He was alone, living in the darkness like a vampire but with no bloodlust to compel him to strive for survival.

He simply existed.

Noah ran through the night until he reached a place that no one else on St. Gabriel Island dared visit…even in the bright, unforgiving light of day.

The concerto of cicadas was very nearly deafening. He drew the thick, balmy air into his lungs, exhaled again and again until his respiration had slowed and his skin had ceased to tingle. A slick coat of sweat had dampened his flesh and he felt cleansed by it.

He moved closer to the looming structure that had

once reigned proudly in the center of a clearing. That clearing had decades ago been reclaimed by the semi-tropical forest. Ivy shrouded the ancient chapel's exterior, hiding the timeworn cracks in its sagging walls, disguising its proximity to inevitable collapse. Inside was cavernous and as dark as a tomb, which was fitting since the rumors on the island had pegged him as the walking dead, a distant cousin of Count Dracula, no doubt.

Some species of the local fauna scurried out through the wide door, open and partially unhinged on one side. Probably a raccoon, Noah decided, unafraid. He waded through knee-deep weeds that grew in the loamy soil as he moved past the chapel and to the cemetery beyond it. He had no fear of anything reptilian or otherwise, he was the walking dead, after all. What did Noah Drake have to fear?

Only the light.

And a past that had destroyed his future, and any semblance of a normal present.

Camouflaged by the creeping flora, primitive headstones, crumbling with age, marked the final resting places of a few of St. Gabriel's former residents. No one on the island ever came near the place anymore. Not since the ground had been tainted some thirty or so years ago by the burial of one of Savannah's premier voodoo queens, or so went the gossip. Noah wondered if the woman had felt as alone in her beliefs as he did in his inescapable isolation.

But he was *alone,* not lonely, he reminded himself. He didn't need anyone. And there was his work…his private expression of aloneness.

Minutes turned into hours as he wandered with no particular destination. He didn't often leave the house for this long, or travel this far from its sanctuary. A simple mistake such as falling and injuring himself could mean certain death if he were unable to return before dawn. But he'd needed to escape the demons from his past and this was the only way he'd known how.

They were coming…for him.

All he could do was wait. It was the waiting that got to him, not the fear for his life. Just the waiting.

Acutely attuned to nature's predawn signals, he eventually moved back toward safety. He slowed as he neared the house. Inside lay reality. Out here, he glanced toward the east and the pink and purple hues already creeping above the horizon, was freedom, hope, possibility.

But his time was up. Going back inside wasn't a mere alternative, it was a necessity. If he remained outdoors and the sun came up, which it would inevitably do…he would die.

As he trudged through the sand, he studied the details of the prison he'd chosen. The three-story Victorian Gothic-style house had a long ways to go before she would be fully restored to her former glory, but she was impressive still, at once brooding and enchanting if one was predisposed to romance.

Hurricane shutters, now closed at all times, masked the floor-to-ceiling windows. More than a century after the house's construction, that detail had become an important one for the new owner. Interior shutters and heavy drapes rendered the numerous massive windows—eyes to the outer world—completely sightless. No one saw in, no one saw out and not even so much as a glimmer of light penetrated his large, aboveground dungeon.

When he reached the screened porch that had been added sometime in the last half of the twentieth century, Noah turned around and looked out over the ocean one last time. That had actually been the deciding factor in his choosing this place. The sound of the surf, the immensity of its boundaries were breathtaking even without the aid of the sun.

It was all that kept him sane.

"Noah, you've been gone for hours." The gently scolding voice greeted him the moment he opened the door into the kitchen.

Tamping down the instant irritation, Noah manufactured a smile for his relentless companion, Lowell Kline. *Companion,* what an odd designation for his mind to conjure, Noah considered abruptly. But it was true. Lowell was paid well to live here, had been for a year now. Did the shopping, the cooking, the laundry, even the cleaning. He fussed over Noah like a grandmother every chance he got. Most of the time Noah avoided him, but sometimes, as now, Lowell would catch Noah off guard and that annoyed him immensely. Lowell wanted to be a true companion in that he wanted to be Noah's friend. But Noah didn't want that. He didn't want anyone to be too close.

"I'm fine, Lowell." He regarded his dedicated employee, wondering again what made him stay. It definitely wasn't the pleasure of the company. Lowell Kline was certainly capable of earning a good wage elsewhere. His still-full head of hair was as white as the clouds Noah remembered from a clear summer's day. Though not a large fellow, at fifty-five Lowell was quite fit. The older man was well-read and deemed himself the resident expert on the island folklore, including the still-secretly-practiced black voodoo and the long-ago days when pirates and smugglers had frequented the place.

"Have you been up all this time?" Noah inquired. He preferred his solitude. Lowell knew that.

Lowell looked flustered. He tried very hard not to let Noah catch him keeping too close tabs. "Well no, but when I awoke and realized you weren't back I began to worry."

Noah nodded, suddenly too tired to discuss the issue. This was his life—existence, he amended. "I apologize if I worried you. Your concern is unnecessary, I assure you. I'm heading for the shower."

"Noah," Lowell said, stalling his departure. "You've received another...*letter.*"

The last word hung in the air like the steamy July humidity outside, only heavy with an undercurrent of apprehension...of menace.

"Let me see." It was only then that Noah noticed Lowell held a bundle of mail under one arm, his reading glasses dangling from his hand. He'd obviously been going through the stack Noah had ignored for the past four days. Noah preferred to do it himself, but whenever he got behind, by choice generally, Lowell took the initiative.

Noah looked at the envelope. As before it was nondescript, white in color, business-size with no return address. The postmark was Atlanta. He reached inside and pulled out the single sheet of paper. It was just like all the others. Letters of the alphabet in different fonts and sizes had been cut from magazines or newspapers and arranged into haphazard words then pasted onto the plain white page.

There's no place to hide.

Noah sighed, crumpled the letter and tossed it across

the room Anger seethed inside him. The letters had been coming once a week for more than two months. The first few had been nothing more than hate mail. That hadn't really bothered him since he'd been called worse by the locals on occasion. But the last three or four had grown threatening. Last week's *I'm coming for you* had sent Lowell over the edge. He'd insisted on informing Edgar Rothman, the only man involved with the government whom Noah even remotely associated with.

Rothman had overreacted as usual.

"There was a call also," Lowell said hesitantly, obviously weighing the merits of saying more but duty bound to do so.

Noah paused again, his fierce glare cut to Lowell, he flinched. "What call?"

"Mr. Rothman wanted you to know that he was sending someone down to…" Lowell cleared his throat. "To serve as a sort of bodyguard."

Noah swore, long and loud, like a sailor fresh in from a long stretch at sea finding his wife in bed with one of the local riffraff. If his enemy wanted revenge, why didn't he take it? These games weren't his style. Either way, Noah wasn't running.

"Call Rothman back and tell him to forget it. I don't want anyone coming here. I will not allow it."

"But, what if—"

Noah pinned him with a look that he felt certain conveyed the finality of his words. "If you would feel more comfortable taking a leave until this is over, I fully understand. But I do not want a damned bodyguard. Under *any* circumstances."

BLUE CALLAHAN surged forward, gaining her second wind as she sprinted into the home stretch of her three-mile run. Her heart pumped hard and steady, forcing the adrenaline-charged blood through her veins and melting the last of the tension from her body.

She'd awakened this morning with a scream trapped in her throat and sweat dampening her skin, nightmares left over from Port Charlotte. The mission had gone smoothly right up until the end. But she'd survived. Vince Ferrelli and Katrina Moore had survived too. The bad guys had been defeated and all was right in the world once more.

Just twenty-four hours had passed and the incident that had shaken her to the core was still fresh in her memory. But it would pass. She knew from experience that it would. Focusing on more pleasant thoughts, she remembered that Lucas Camp had mentioned that he had scheduled a mission where she would be the primary. He'd also warned that there was a short fuse on this one, she should be ready ASAP.

She was ready.

As soon as she had shaken off the lingering effects of the nightmare, she'd started packing in preparation. She didn't have to know where she was going or for how long; all Specialists were trained on the proper preparations for a mission. Her selections would cover most any situation or climate.

Then she'd pushed, stretching to her physical limits all morning in an effort to dispel the remnants of the nightmares. Glancing at her watch, she realized it was almost noon and she was starved.

If she hurried she could make it to Terry's Pizza in time for lunch with the usual crew. Blue bounded away from the track, slowing her pace as she approached the gym. This training facility was for Specialists only. Every person here was assigned to the most highly covert organization belonging to the United States government. Blue's unit, Special Operations, fell under Mission Recovery and was headed by Director Thomas Casey. Lucas Camp, one of her favorite people, served as Deputy Director.

This state-of-the-art training facility made the FBI's Farm look like an elementary-school playground. Blue smiled at that thought. She'd considered a career at the Bureau first when she graduated from UCLA, but she'd chosen the Secret Service instead. Having hailed from a family of cops, third generation at that, she had definitely wanted to go into law enforcement. But being the only girl in her close-knit family of six siblings, Blue had learned hard and fast that if she didn't keep one step ahead of the boys, she'd always be two steps behind. So she'd opted for federal service rather than local law enforcement. Being asked for by name by the president himself had made her a legend in the Callahan family as well as envied by her peers.

No one in her family could believe it when she had left the Secret Service for her current duty. Forward Research, the people whose sole responsibility was to scout out talent for Mission Recovery, had noticed her Secret Service exploits and, the moment the president for whom she worked had left office, they'd lured her away from the dark suits and designer sunglasses.

Mission Recovery's whole cloak-and-dagger routine had seduced her. Now her brothers, all local cops in L.A., were permanently one-upped. Little sister was a secret agent. She always laughed and told them it was nothing nearly so James Bondish as all that. But the truth was, they were closer to the mark than they knew.

Mission Recovery had been created to serve the needs of all other government agencies, CIA, FBI, ATF, DEA. Whenever the usual channels failed, Mission Recovery was called in to "recover" the situation. Blue could vouch for the fact that all the members of this elite group, called Specialists, were highly trained in all areas of anti-terrorism, aggressive infiltration and such. Of course, she couldn't share any of that with her brothers.

But that was okay with Blue. She didn't do any of it for the notoriety, she did it because she loved the job. Most of the time anyway.

She slowed to a walk as she entered the gym and made the journey to the women's locker rooms. The place was deserted. There weren't that many females in Mission Recovery, but their facilities were every bit as elaborate as their male counterparts'.

Peeling off her T-shirt, she toed off her sneakers, then reached for the door to her locker. Her cellular telephone rang. She flipped down the mouthpiece and said a breathless, "Callahan."

"Blue, this is Joan at the gallery."

Blue's heart did a somersault. "Hey, Joan." She tried to stay calm and not jump the gun here, but adrenaline was already soaring through her.

"I've located another painting by that obscure artist."

"So I can purchase the one I've been admiring?" she asked quickly. She had to know! She'd mooned—obsessed really—over that painting for months now. She'd even dreamed of the enigmatic artist behind the work. Too bad no one, not even the gallery owner, knew his name. The work was simply signed N.D.D. All transactions were conducted through his agent.

N.D.D. was a complete mystery. One Blue would like nothing better than to solve. Since his work was so hard to come by, the gallery owner was reluctant to let it go.

Joan laughed softly. ''Drop by at your convenience. I'll be holding it for you.''

Blue tossed the phone back into the locker and did a little victory dance. The painting was hers. Thoughts of the dark, sensual images of the almost Gothic-looking forest scene made her shiver. And now it was hers!

She snagged her towel. Maybe she'd have time to pick it up today. Clad only in her sports bra and running shorts, she closed her locker and turned to head toward the showers.

She inhaled sharply at the sight of Lucas Camp sitting on a bench at the end of the row of lockers, a briefcase at his feet.

''Afternoon, Callahan.'' He propped his hands on his cane and eyed her unapologetically. ''I hope this isn't a bad time.''

''No, sir.'' Growing up with five brothers made a girl pretty damned unflappable. She threw the towel over her shoulder and moved to the bench. ''Your timing is perfect. I've been thinking about you and that assignment you mentioned.'' She sat down next to him.

Though the last place she'd expected to receive a mission briefing was in the women's locker room at the training facility, she'd waited a long time to be the primary on an assignment. She'd take it any way it came. No matter that her record with the Secret Service was stellar, all Specialists started out on the same level and had to earn their way in Mission Recovery.

Impressing the likes of Lucas Camp and Thomas Casey was no easy feat.

Lucas reached into his briefcase and brought out a large unmarked manila envelope. "Here's the profile on your principal, Noah Drake. You'll serve as his personal bodyguard until further notice."

Blue nodded. "I look forward to the opportunity."

Those wise gray eyes studied her for several seconds before he continued. "Mr. Drake has special circumstances." Lucas nodded toward the envelope. "The necessary details are there. To cut to the chase, before forced retirement as a major in military intelligence he was instrumental in numerous high-level missions. It would be pointless to tell you the branch he served since our government continues to deny its existence, it suffices to say that its chief focus is research and development and Major Drake was one of their best-kept secrets."

Blue listened intently, her heart surging into a brisk pace once more. This sounded like a choice assignment.

"Five years ago Drake volunteered to test their newest prototype." Lucas drew in a deep breath, then let it go as if taking the time to consider his next words more carefully. "The new technology appeared successful and was used in an operation that brought down a ring of traitors within our own government.

"Unfortunately two things went wrong," Lucas resumed after a moment's pause. "There was a serious discrepancy in a piece of crucial evidence and the ring leader, General Regan Bonner, got off with a mere slap on the hand, four years in a minimum-security institution. Club Med, if you get my drift."

A frown worried Blue's brow as she waited for the

rest. When his pause lengthened, she prompted, "You said two things went wrong."

Lucas nodded, his expression solemn. "The experimental technology had an adverse effect on Noah Drake's physical health. He had to give up his career and live like a prisoner in his own home. And that's where he remains to this day."

"So Bonner has been released and he represents a threat to Drake?"

"We believe that to be the case. Bonner swore he would have his vengeance on Drake. And since his release six months ago, intel suggests that he has not only behaved suspiciously, but that he has been consorting with known assassins and other anti-American partisans. Then two months ago, Drake started receiving threatening letters."

Blue unconsciously dragged loose the holder from her ponytail in preparation for that badly needed shower, but her thoughts were on Drake. "Where is Drake now?"

"Are you familiar with St. Gabriel Island?"

She shook her head.

"It's just off the coast of Georgia," he explained. "Near Savannah. That's where you'll fly into. We've chartered a boat to take you to the island. Once there, transportation will be provided."

Picturing a tropical island, Blue said, "Sounds like a vacation spot."

"It's a lovely place, that's true enough," Lucas told her as if he had firsthand knowledge. "But it's small and the locals don't care much for outsiders. They'll shun you, probably make you feel completely unwanted. Since you won't be there to make friends, that won't really matter. Just don't expect to be embraced as if you were on a more touristy island.''

''When do I leave?'' Adrenaline spiked. She was so ready for this.

''Your flight to Atlanta and then on to Savannah leaves National tomorrow morning. Can you handle that?''

Blue smiled. ''I started packing this morning in anticipation of your call.'' That still gave her time to pick up the painting.

Though Lucas didn't smile, she didn't miss the sparkle of amusement and approval in his eyes. ''Very good, Callahan. The other accessories you'll need will be waiting on St. Gabriel.''

Blue knew what he meant by ''other accessories.'' When flying commercial it was always best to have the weapons one needed waiting on the other end. It cut down on the hassle and supported anonymity.

''Who's got my back?'' she asked, wondering if it would be someone she had supported before.

Lucas didn't answer for a moment, just considered her as if trying to decide if she was ready to hear what he had to say. ''That's why I came down here instead of calling you into the office.''

She'd wondered about that, but was so glad to get the assignment she didn't question the irregularity.

''Edgar Rothman,'' Lucas continued, ''is a personal friend of Director Casey's. Rothman feels personally responsible for what happened to Drake since he was the one who created the technology used. He doesn't want just anyone looking out for Drake. Rothman wants the best. So, I'm sending you. I'll have your back on this one.''

Blue's eyes rounded in disbelief. ''*You'll* be on St.

Gabriel?'' She'd heard the words clearly enough, it just didn't seem plausible that she'd heard correctly.

"Don't worry, Callahan.'' Lucas did smile this time. "I might spend most of my time behind a desk, but I know what I'm doing.''

She forced her head into an agreeable up-and-down motion. She didn't doubt his qualifications or his ability. The idea was just a little unnerving. "Yes, sir.''

Lucas pushed to his feet and reached for his briefcase. "Well, I'll leave you to carry on, my flight is this afternoon.''

Callahan followed him to the door. "Thanks, Mr. Camp.''

Lucas patted her on the arm the same way her father had done a thousand times. "Don't worry, Callahan, I don't bite, and, to the best of my knowledge, neither does Drake. Don't be afraid to act as you would under any other circumstances. I won't be there to rate your performance, I'll be there as the director's personal representative.''

Callahan didn't move for a long time after the door closed behind Lucas Camp. Sure it made her a tad uneasy to know that the boss was going to be watching her every step. But as far as being afraid went, she definitely wasn't.

Blue Callahan wasn't afraid of anything.

A telling stillness crept through her.

Okay. There was that one itsy-bitsy matter but it didn't really count. And no one except Ferrelli knew about it.

Her entire life she had been utterly terrified of one thing and one thing only—*the dark.*

Chapter Two

Unfortunately the stifling humidity she'd encountered the moment she stepped off the plane in Atlanta hadn't abated as Blue made the boat ride to St. Gabriel Island late that evening. The view, even in the coming twilight, she had to admit, was nothing short of spectacular. She'd have been here hours ago had it not been for baggage-check delays in Atlanta.

As they cut through the water's sleek surface, she inhaled more deeply of the salty wind caressing her face. It was rich with scents, nothing like the kind she was accustomed to in the big city. Admittedly, there was a vague hint of decaying vegetation and fish, but it wasn't an overpowering smell, more a dash of aroma one would expect in the vicinity of a sea island.

As the boat slowed near the landing, Blue studied the small island. Near the aging dock, which served as a primitive marina, she could see what looked like a small commercial district. Very small, she decided on second look and *commercial* applied only in the most obscure sense of the word. Towering trees dripping Spanish moss from their arching limbs lined the sandy shore, sentinels guarding the forest beyond, a forest that looked incredibly deep and dark. She resisted the urge to shiver. And yet, it felt oddly familiar. She frowned, wondering at the sensation. She'd certainly never been here before.

It wasn't what Blue had expected at all. When Lucas had said *island,* she'd thought of palm trees and other tropical plants, beaches filled with sunbathers and at least a few tourist hangouts. Not for a moment had she expected evergreens, live oaks and other deciduous trees with gnarled branches. And she definitely hadn't anticipated the apparently sparse population.

In spite of her best efforts that shiver she'd put off tap-danced up her spine. She was being ridiculous, she knew. But all things considered, the whole mission was a little eerie even without the seemingly deserted island setting.

She'd studied the profile on Noah Drake. He was thirty-five, former military and highly decorated. Five years ago he'd field-tested some sort of experimental technology that was not explained since it was highly classified and explanations were doled out on a need-to-know basis only. The brass had apparently decided she didn't need to know specifically what the technology was or what exactly were the resulting effects as applied to Mr. Drake. Nothing like going in blind.

She did know, however, that Drake had suffered extreme side effects. There was no mention of a physical disability, but that didn't rule it out. He was confined to his home and had to avoid exposure to bright light, especially sunlight, at all costs. She decided that his eyes were likely the problem. Maybe his skin. Whatever the case, she would soon know.

The bottom line—and her only real concern at this point—was that he needed protection. And she was here to provide it. Noah Drake would be safe on her watch.

The boat sidled up alongside the rustic dock and Blue climbed out. She was glad now she'd dressed in jeans and walking shoes. The jeans were faded and comfortable and the black button-up blouse was her favorite.

The pilot plopped the two duffel bags she'd packed onto the worn planks. Blue thanked him and turned toward the shore. She shaded her eyes from the setting sun with her hand and searched the landing for the transportation Lucas had told her would be waiting.

An ancient pickup truck was parked about fifty feet back from the beach. At one time the vehicle appeared to have been some shade of green, though it was hard to say for sure now. Blue grabbed up her bags and started in that direction.

As she neared him, the thin man standing next to the truck pushed back his cap and scratched his balding head. "Miss Callahan?"

"At your service," she responded, smiling a greeting in hopes of getting off on the right foot with the locals.

"Chester Parks." He spat tobacco juice onto the ground, then squinted at her. "I'm s'posed to take you to the old Hatfield place."

"That would be Mr. Drake's residence?" she asked for clarification.

Reaching for one of her bags, Chester spat again and said, "Yeah. Long time ago it was a sugar plantation run by the Hatfields. Guess the name just stuck."

Blue nodded her understanding and handed him the other bag once he'd tossed the first one into the back of his truck. Maybe the islanders weren't as standoffish as Lucas thought. This guy seemed friendly enough.

"I'm eager to meet Mr. Drake," she told him.

The second bag plopped down next to the first. Chester eyed her skeptically. "I imagine you'd be the only one eager for his company around here."

Keeping the frown out of her expression, she prodded, "Why is that?"

"Well, I don't mean to speak ill of nobody, specially if he's your kin, but he's an odd sort." Chester rounded the tailgate to the driver's side and opened the door, but hesitated before getting in. "He roams around all hours of the night like some kinda vampire. He don't have no visitors 'cept that Mr. Kline. And—" Chester looked at her as if this was the gravest part of all "—he goes places God-fearing folks don't go. Guess you'll have to see for yourself."

Blue slid into the passenger seat and wondered if Chester's sentiments toward Mr. Drake were common among the residents. She supposed they didn't understand his condition or the reclusiveness it dictated. It wasn't her place to explain the circumstances. Drake might prefer his privacy.

Now that she'd had a chance to take a closer look, she noted that the "commercial district" offerings were as scarce as the population around here appeared to be. A bar, BullDog's, and a large metal warehouse that advertised bicycle and what looked like golf cart rentals by the hour or day was just about the extent of it.

"There ain't that many vehicles on the island," Chester said when he followed her gaze to the golf carts. "Most folks walk or ride bicycles. Since I've got ol' Bessy here, I run errands for Mr. Kline and a few of the other shut-ins. Been doing it ever since I came back from the navy in '59.''

Blue acknowledged his chitchat with noncommittal sounds and nods at the appropriate times. She'd learned long ago that one gleaned far more by listening. Chester would know the island gossip, so she allowed him to ramble on without interruption. There was no more talk about vampires, but pirates and smugglers appeared to be a big part of the island lore.

He'd mentioned Mr. Kline. Lowell Kline had been Noah Drake's sole associate for the past year. That much had been in the report. No one else was allowed in the house. Chester had called him a shut-in. That led Blue to wonder if Mr. Kline ever left the house either. Blue couldn't bear that kind of lonely existence. She loved feeling the wind in her hair and the sun on her face too well. She was a California girl through and through.

Chester shifted into reverse, the transmission grinding in loud protest, and turned around so that the truck pointed toward the one road.

Blue blinked, thinking she had to be wrong, then looked again. Yep, just one road.

''Most visitors rent a cart,'' Chester rattled on. ''They're right handy for getting you where you're going around here. Not that there's that much to do or see. Most tourists flock to St. Simons or Tybee Island. We don't see many of 'em here. Just a few curious Georges now and again wanting to see some of the old caves the smugglers once used.''

Forcing interest into her expression and uneasiness out of it, she nodded. ''I guess it's always this quiet around here then.''

"We like it that way." He glanced in her direction as he shifted into second. "You'll get used to it."

Not wanting to hurt his feelings, she smiled and kept her thoughts on the matter to herself: *not in this lifetime.*

Jimmy Buffet's "Cheeseburger in Paradise" emanated from somewhere, the bar maybe. She studied the joint as they chugged past it. To a degree it defied description, the kind term would be *quaint.* In Blue's estimation it was a dump. A shack with a rusty corrugated tin roof and a couple of windows that had been boarded shut at one time or another. There was no way to tell if the damage had been caused by a storm or by rowdy patrons. Beer logos and a crude hand-painted sign displaying the hours of business decorated the weathered batten-board siding. One truck, a relative of the one Chester drove no doubt, two bicycles and a moped were parked in front of the establishment. Things were jumping at BullDog's, she mused.

At the edge of "downtown" was a small general store, its dusty parking area empty. The building wasn't large, but it was well-maintained, clean even. As they drove by, an elderly man stepped onto the stoop, broom in hand, and vigorously swept off the steps.

"That's where most folks get the little things they run out of now and again." Chester nodded toward Weber's Grocery. "Gotta go to the mainland to get your staples though. O'Mally, the fella who hauled you over, makes two runs a day from the mainland, once in the morning, once in the evening. Otherwise you gotta hire some local to run you back and forth."

Blue had lived in one major city or the other her

whole life. This was definitely a big change. No carry-out pizza, no taco stands, no Chinese takeout, no nothing.

She shook her head and amended her thinking. No, this wasn't a big change. This was a whole different planet. Lucas had failed to mention that little detail.

The woods bordered the narrow island road for as far as Blue could see in the enveloping gloom. And, as far as she could tell, there really was only the one road, which was as bumpy as all get out. Alongside the cramped road, undergrowth was thick, the massive canopy of the trees stretching over it blocking the sun's waning light.

She didn't like the dark. She stiffened her spine and tamped down the budding fear. It wasn't completely dark, she reminded herself, just gloomy. She'd be at her destination before darkness completely descended.

But one thing was a given, she wouldn't want to be out in these woods at night. No way. She couldn't shake the sensation of recognition, though she knew it was not feasible.

Occasionally she noticed what looked like a side road, but the foliage worked as such good camouflage that she couldn't be sure if she'd seen anything at all. She hadn't noticed a single house or person except for the handful of patrons at the bar and general store, and, of course, Chester.

"Here we go."

Chester turned right, bouncing down a lane that was one pothole after the other. The woods closed in on Blue now, dark, silent and subliminally threatening. Her uneasiness escalated in spite of her conscious efforts to keep it in check.

Get a grip, she chastised herself. She might be a fish

out of water in these surroundings, but she could adapt. Give her a flashlight and a nine-millimeter and she could kick anybody's butt, even in the dark.

Finally the near-nonexistent road widened slightly. A tall wrought-iron gate crossed their path. Hinged on brick pillars that stood on either side of the lane, one side of the ornate gate was open, allowing their passage. Beyond the apparently decorative feature the compact undergrowth and the dense forest opened up into a clearing. A lush green lawn stretched for half an acre and stopped abruptly at the foundation of a towering three-story house. Blue wasn't that up to speed on this particular architecture, but it looked old, as in antique-old—mid-1800s, if she had to guess. And a little like something from an Emily Brontë novel with its perception of beauty marred by a distinct air of evil, especially in the fading light.

Ivy carpeted a great deal of the brick exterior. Here and there resurrection fern sprouted from a crack in the centuries-old mortar. Window after window— long, wide windows—were shut tight with hurricane shutters. A crenelated tower and a parapet along the tin-shingled roofline lent a castle-like feel to the place. Wooden icicles of fretwork and other intricately carved ornamentation softened the hard exterior.

A wide verandah sprawled across the front of the house, twilight casting it in long shadows. A smaller balcony centered on the second floor. The third floor of the structure, the tower, could have been a fairy-tale turret had it been round instead of square. A tower room, she decided, feeling suddenly better. Okay, she could live with that. When she'd been a little girl she'd dreamed of being a princess and living in a castle. Her fantasy chamber had been at the very top of the spiral stairs. The tower room. She smiled faintly at the memory. She wasn't a little girl anymore and she darned sure wasn't a princess. Far from it. But this was nice. A little too far away from civilization, but doable on a temporary basis.

The house looked in fairly good condition, maintenancewise. But there was something unsettling about it, she decided the moment Chester turned off the truck's engine. It was so quiet. The shutters were closed tight over the numerous windows. Another shameful waste of architectural beauty. She supposed it was Drake's condition that necessitated the closed shutters. She swiped at her damp brow with the back of her hand and hoped there was air-conditioning. It was still hot and sticky and the sun was all but gone from sight.

As she emerged from the truck, bottles hanging from a nearby tree captured her attention. "What're those?" she asked, closing the door behind her and pointing to the bottles in question.

Chester flicked a glance toward the tree. "Spirit bottles," he said. "They keep the evil spirits away."

The breeze shifted the bottles, stirring to life a clanging noise that made her shiver all over again.

"Way I hear it, they don't do much good around here." Chester reached for her bags and led the way up the eight steps that divided the house from the lawn.

She opted not to pursue the subject of the spirit bottles. Blue had never been superstitious, nor did she believe in any of the related mumbo-jumbo. She wasn't about to start now.

Before they'd crossed the verandah, the intricately carved mahogany door opened wide.

"Thank you, Chester," the man standing in the doorway, Mr. Kline, she presumed, said as he stepped back for Chester to place her bags just inside the house.

Chester touched the tip of his hat. "See you on Friday." As he turned to leave, his gaze caught Blue's and held for just one second. She couldn't decipher the look in his eyes, sympathy maybe, before he walked away.

"Miss Callahan, I'm glad you're here."

Blue turned her attention back to the older, white-haired man waiting at the door. He had the same drawl as Chester, only a bit more distinguished. He was dressed in khaki slacks and a crisp white shirt and reminded her of a professor she'd once had. "Mr. Kline?"

He thrust out his hand. "Call me Lowell, please." He gave her hand a quick, polite shake, then gestured inside. "Won't you come in?"

To her immense relief, climate-controlled air greeted her as Blue crossed the threshold. Lowell closed the door behind her and—

It was dark.

She stopped dead in her tracks, her heart jolted into a faster rhythm.

"Why are the lights so low?" There was no way to miss the edge of panic in her voice. She swallowed at the rising sensation, and blinked rapidly to force her eyes to adjust.

"I'm afraid it's something you'll need to get used to, Miss Callahan. With Mr. Drake's condition, the wattage allowed in any room is minimal."

She peered at Kline in the dim light and hoped he couldn't see the level of her disbelief as she pointed to the fixture. "This is hardly more than a beefed-up night-light."

He sighed. "I'm afraid so. Didn't anyone tell you?"

"Sure." She plastered a smile into place. All she needed was for this guy to report back that she was uncomfortable with the conditions. "I guess it's just a little…" She shrugged. "A little darker than I expected." A *lot* darker than she'd expected.

"Your vision will adjust." He picked up her bags before she could protest and moved toward the graceful stairs that ascended from the middle of the center hall to the second-story landing. "We'll take your things up to your room so you can get settled."

Forcing herself to relax, Blue's gaze moved appreciatively over the elegant staircase. The details were obscured but looked impressive by any standards. A red or burgundy carpet runner on the wooden treads kept their footfalls silent as she followed Lowell up the stairs. He led her to the first room on the right. There were three other doors that she could see. She peered toward the far end of the hall where a second smaller staircase led to the third floor. A dozen questions about the house as well as its owner sprang to mind, but they could wait.

After depositing her bags onto the bed, Lowell indicated a door across the room. A bathroom probably. "When you've settled in and freshened up, come downstairs and I'll serve your dinner."

"That would be nice." She hadn't bothered with lunch at the crowded airport. She'd been too psyched and ready to begin her assignment.

"Before I forget." Lowell reached into the pocket of his trousers and produced a key. He looked at it for a long moment, as if hesitant, then offered it to Blue. "This is the key to the house."

She took it, glanced at it briefly, then lifted her gaze back to his as he added, "The exterior doors and windows are locked at all times. Never," he pressed her with a gaze at once intense and beseeching, "ever leave one open or unlocked." He cleared his throat. "The drapes and shutters are to remain closed at all times and no other light, not even a flashlight, is allowed. The third floor is off limits."

She nodded. "I understand."

His gaze was relentless now. He reminded Blue of a bear guarding her only surviving cub. He apparently needed to be absolutely certain she understood. "I don't know how much you've been told about Mr. Drake's condition, but mere minutes in bright light would kill him. For that reason, no one is allowed in the house other than myself and now you."

"There's no need for concern, Mr. Kli—Lowell," she amended. "Though I don't know all the specifics, I can assure you that I won't do anything that will jeopardize Mr. Drake in any way." This was her first big assignment, she had every intention of impressing the brass. But it would certainly help if she knew more particulars about Drake. She'd have to bide her time it seemed.

Lowell nodded, looking contrite. "Of course. If you have any other questions, don't hesitate to ask." He paused at the door. "I almost forgot. There's a case for you on the bureau." He gestured to a massive piece of furniture near the heavily draped windows. "It was delivered yesterday." He said it as if knowing what the case contained and finding it more than a little distasteful.

"One question." Blue stopped him before he could get out the door. "When can I meet Mr. Drake?"

"I'm sorry, Miss Callahan." His posture grew more rigid.

"Call me Blue," she echoed his earlier words, hoping to penetrate the wall he'd suddenly thrown up.

"Blue," he acquiesced, "I'm afraid Mr. Drake usually doesn't leave his room until well after sunset. Even then he prefers his solitude. But I'm sure he'll want to meet with you in time. Is there anything else I can do for you?"

In time? Blue pushed the disappointment away. She liked to get the feel of her assignment as quickly as possible, but pushing the subject wouldn't help. She had to gain trust here. She needed to know Drake's routine, his likes and dislikes. What he expected of her.

"No." She shrugged as if considering her other options. "I can't think of anything else I need at the moment. I'll get settled and maybe do a little exploring before it gets too dark."

"Very good." He hesitated once more before leaving. "There is one other thing."

She looked at him expectantly, waiting for yet another revelation that would hinder her ability to do her job.

"Mr. Drake isn't pleased about this. He didn't want protection. The fact of the matter is I've gone directly against his wishes allowing you here. I'm not sure your first meeting with him will be pleasant."

Perfect. Blue smiled in hopes of relieving his evident anxiety and not giving away her own. "Not to worry. I have five ornery older brothers at home. I'm pretty good at handling that kind of macho male mentality.''

Lowell's uncertain expression remained in place, but, to his credit, he attempted a smile. ''Well, I'll see you in a bit then.''

Blue watched him go, then slowly surveyed the spacious room with its high ceilings and period furnishings. Plain, drab, and what she decided had to be beige walls and beige bed coverings. It was hard to say for certain in the low light. No pictures or other decorating items. Judging by the room's size, she thought it might be what was considered the master suite. A quick look into the adjoining bathroom and she was sure of it.

She exhaled a weary breath and wondered how the heck she was supposed to do her job if Drake didn't want her here? She lifted her chin and folded her arms over her chest. Easy, she decided. She'd just have to change his mind. She had a lifetime of experience charming the male of the species.

It only took Blue a few minutes to unpack her things and check out the weapons Lucas had arranged for her use. She strapped on the ankle holster, pulled her jeans leg down over it, then shrugged into her shoulder holster before going downstairs. She always felt naked without her gun. Throughout her whole life, the people she loved most had accessorized with weapons. Well, except for her mother, who'd crossed herself every time one of them walked in or out of a room carrying a gun. Though she had little tolerance for violence, Margaret Callahan was as tough as nails. She'd had to be to survive in the same house with that many cop egos.

Blue checked out the other three rooms on the second floor. All were bedrooms, one looked to be

Lowell's. Each room was as large as hers and had its own private bath. And all were dull-as-dirt beige. Lowell had hung a few pictures, of family or friends, she supposed, and on one wall was a large Georgia Bull Dogs banner. A small television set occupied the far corner. She wondered if the island had cable. Probably not.

She resisted the urge to check out the third floor. It was off limits, Lowell had said. Judging by its size, as seen from outside, Mr. Drake's suite most likely made up the entire floor. He was probably sleeping up there right now. She shook off the vampirish images that formed in her head as she recalled Chester's remark about the reclusive man. Time to get the lay of the land.

Her hand glided along the curved banister as she slowly descended the staircase. For the first time she noticed the finer details of the huge chandelier that hung above the center hall. It was lovely, dimly lit, but lovely just the same.

She wondered vaguely if the electrical wiring had been modified or if the lights themselves had been changed in some way to ensure that the light wattage remained so low. Though her eyes were already beginning to adjust as Lowell had said they would, it was still too dark for her liking.

But she'd deal with it.

The main parlor was just as plain and beige as the rest of the rooms. Not that she had anything against beige, mind you. But this beige monotony was unbroken by anything other than wood floors and wood trim, all the color of rich, dark coffee, like the mahogany door on the front of the house. She considered that maybe white was too reflective and most other colors too dark, thus the selection of beige. Maybe she'd ask about that. Eventually.

Thankfully the parlor's furnishings were more contemporary and slightly more colorful. There was another television set and a stereo system. Someone liked classical music, she decided, noting the stack of CDs. A desk and computer along with row after row of book-filled shelves occupied one side of the room. Like the rest of the house, the windows were shrouded in thick draperies—even they were beige. But at least this room looked used. The brown leather sofa looked worn and comfortable and was flanked by two plaid overstuffed side chairs.

As she strayed back into the hall a whiff of something absolutely heavenly enticed her nose and made her stomach rumble. She followed the delicious scent to the kitchen at the rear of the house.

"Whatever that is, it smells great," she commented aloud.

Lowell glanced up from the oven. "Ten more minutes and you'll find out." He closed the door and laid the oven mitt aside. "It's my own secret recipe."

Blue smiled at the note of camaraderie in his tone. "Can't wait." She took in the kitchen in one sweep. Modern, but not so much that it took away from the house's overall feel of a bygone era. "I think I'll take a walk and get my bearings," she announced, feeling restless and with a definite need to see the sun one last time before it disappeared for the day, leaving her to this gloom.

He nodded absently. "Don't be long."

Blue was careful to lock the front door behind her just as Lowell had instructed. Taking her time, she surveyed the grounds around the front of the house.

The spirit bottles jangled as the breeze kicked up, drawing her attention or maybe warning her of some impending doom. She grinned and wondered if Lowell had done that, or maybe Mr. Drake under the cover of darkness just to spook the locals. But surely neither of them would be the superstitious type.

As she strolled around the house she was caught off guard again by the dark, foreboding forest that closed in on the yard from both sides. Trees, centuries old and laden with moss, towered over the thick brambles and undergrowth that cloaked all else. The distant rustle of leaves startled her, sent her backing up several steps. She executed a quick right face and marched to the backyard.

Pete's sake, she was too old for this kind of childish behavior.

The moment she rounded the corner at the back of the house, her breath caught. The beach flowed right up to the grass, less than twenty yards from the house. The blue surf foamed white, roared and then died on the sand, dragging back only to start the whole process over again. All but a sliver of the sun had melted into the horizon, leaving vivid streaks of gold and orange to color the otherwise royal-blue sky. She closed her eyes and inhaled the salty air.

She wished she was barefoot as she walked through the sand, but she was on the job. She looked back at the house. God, it was beautiful. A wide screened porch had been added for enjoying the view of the Atlantic. A widow's walk loomed high overhead. She wondered if anxious wives had used it as a lookout for their husbands returning from the sea. Or maybe the pirates and smugglers had benefited from the perfect vantage.

Blue was certain she'd never seen any place more beautiful.

Despite the darkness that lay within those walls, she couldn't call this place unappealing. It was no wonder Mr. Drake had chosen this island, this house as his refuge.

She turned to look out over the ocean once more, chafing her arms to chase away the tremble that accompanied the knowledge that the sun was now completely gone.

She stalled mid-turn.

A thread of tension tightened inside her.

Someone was watching her.

Chapter Three

Blue stared up at the third-story tower room as the tension erupted into a shiver that raced across her skin. She braced herself against the sensation, but it didn't help.

Someone was watching her.

Was it him?

Drake?

The last rays of the sun sank beneath the horizon, slinking away with the waning light and leaving nothing but the gray of desolate dusk as she stood on the beach and peered up at the house through the thickening gloom.

"I'm not so easy to spook, Drake," she muttered. "So don't be thinking you can be rid of me so simply." Lowell had warned her that Drake didn't want her here.

She would change his mind. Surely common sense would prevail. If the man's life was in danger, he needed protection. His enemy could strike at any moment.

A crack ruptured the silence.

Blue recognized it instantly.

Gunshot. High-powered rifle.

The sand kicked up where the next round pierced it. She dove for cover. There was none.

Simultaneously unholstering her weapon and scrambling toward the edge of the forest, Blue kept her head low as yet another shot rang out and plowed into the ground less than three feet away.

A hunter, she considered.

Not open season if things on the island were consistent with those on the mainland.

The shots hadn't come from the direction of the house. Not likely from Drake. At least she hoped liked hell it wasn't him. Then again, he could be over the edge.

As soon as she'd reached the fringes of the forest, she stilled, listening for telltale sounds of the approaching shooter.

Silence.

Long minutes passed as she moved deeper into the concealing shadows of the forest, her ears ever alert for sound, her gaze moving constantly in search of movement. There was no time to think, only to act.

She needed to work her way around to the front of the house and then use the overgrown shrubs for cover to cross the lawn. Getting inside and checking on Drake was top priority.

He could be in danger.

This little game of carnival shooting gallery could be nothing more than a distraction to keep her occupied while the real trouble went down inside.

Lowell kept the house locked. That was good. But it wouldn't stop an assassin intent on accomplishing his mission.

She kept moving, adrenaline urging her forward. The undergrowth was thick…the brambles unforgiving. She pushed through the brush, trying not to think about what might be hiding within its concealing depths.

As the threat appeared to lessen, she slowly became aware of her surroundings. Complete darkness had closed in around her.

Her heart thundered in reaction, sending the sting of panic rushing through her torso...her limbs. Her hands shook. Sweat dampened her skin. She had to keep going.

...I wouldn't want to be out in these woods at night. The memory of the very words she'd thought only a couple of hours ago slammed into her head.

And here you are, another little voice taunted.

Blue muttered a curse. She reached beneath her button-up shirt and shook the light stick hanging on her chain. The black color of her shirt kept the glow hidden, but it was there and that's all that mattered. She could make the dark go away if only a little. Instantly her heart rate dropped to a more normal pace.

Moving cautiously, she was almost to the front of the house. No more shots had been fired and she hadn't sensed any signs of a tail. Maybe it was some local goofing off with target practice. If that was the case someone needed to instruct him on weapon safety. Those shots had been all too close for comfort. On second thought, Blue decided the guy needed his butt kicked L.A. style.

A twig snapped maybe ten yards behind her.

She stopped. Held her breath. Listened intently. And squinted into the consuming darkness without moving a muscle. There was something...

A whisper of foliage against fabric or maybe skin tingled her auditory senses.

He was closer…almost on top of her.

She darted to her right, then ran like hell, hoping to God she wouldn't crash into a tree.

The light from the full moon pierced the thick overhead canopy from time to time, just enough to give her some sense of place and direction. A silent mantra trembled on her lips over and over keeping her focused. *I'm not afraid of the dark. I'm not afraid of the dark.* She had her gun and her light. They were all she needed.

In spite of the blood pounding in her brain and the occasional crashing sounds made by her plunge through the dense vegetation, every now and then she heard a snap or a rustle of underbrush behind her.

He was coming.

Harder, faster she surged forward, low-lying branches snagged at her clothes, her skin, like long bony fingers from the stone-cold hand of death.

Her shoe snagged on a root. She pitched forward and barely caught herself before she hit the ground.

He was almost on top of her now.

She pushed onward. Her lungs were beginning to burn for more oxygen. She couldn't control her breathing anymore. Had to breathe deeper, faster. Had to have more air. What the hell? She was already making more than enough noise to give herself away.

She burst into a clearing, thigh-deep weeds and brush slapping at her jeans.

A shaft of moonlight glinted off something large…a building.

Blue lunged for it and took cover inside. A dank, musty odor immediately shrouded her. She crouched down, her weapon clenched in one hand as she braced the other on the floor for support while she caught her breath. She didn't even want to know what the furry stuff under her fingers was. Moss maybe. She could hope.

She held her breath, released it slowly. Willed her heart rate to decrease. Forced her mind to focus on the impending threat…to pinpoint the direction and proximity. He couldn't be far away.

Listening intently, analyzing each sound, she heard nothing but the resonance of the night bearing down on her.

The constant cry of cicadas.

The wind stirring the leaves.

Damn, it was dark.

She made herself as small as possible, hunkering in the blackness just inside the open doorway, her weapon leveled steadily in her right hand, her left hand now flattened against her chest, feeling for the small light stick beneath her shirt and drawing comfort as her fingers closed around it.

He moved.

She didn't hear him and certainly didn't see him, but she sensed the movement.

To her right…five yards away maybe.

She squinted in that direction and saw nothing. He couldn't be that close. If he'd left the cover of the trees, she should have seen at least a glimpse of him or a glimmer of movement in the moonlight.

…*roams around all hours of the night like some kindda vampire*… Chester's words echoed.

Glass jangled, jerking her gaze to the left.

Spirit bottles like the ones back at the house hung from the lowest limb of a nearby live oak. The bottles swayed, banging against each other from time to time, the moonlight glinting from their surfaces. A new kind of uneasiness slid through her and she called herself every kind of fool. She was not superstitious. And she damn sure didn't believe in vampires.

The deep weeds rustled, yielding beneath a heavy footstep.

She looked right again, her heart jolting back into top speed.

Nothing.

There was nothing there.

Dammit.

There had to be.

''It's safe to come out now, Maggie Callahan.''

Her heart skidded to a near-stop at the sound of the deep, male voice splitting the darkness, drowning out all other sound with its richness...its seeming oneness with the night.

''Whoever was shooting is gone now. You don't have to be afraid.''

She blinked, peered as hard as she could in the direction of the voice, but saw nothing. She swore silently.

''Come out, Maggie Callahan,'' he said, an underlying amusement in his silky tone now. She could almost see him smiling. ''Let me show you the way back to the house before you stumble over something that bites.''

She gritted her teeth against a shudder. Who the hell was this guy? It wasn't Lowell or Chester. There was a slight, ever so slight, drawl, but the voice was too deep and smooth to belong to either of them. It could be Drake, she considered, but she couldn't imagine him running out into the darkness like this since his life was in danger already.

Not unless he'd lost his mind anyway.

"Who are you?" she demanded, giving away her position but seeing no way around it. She darted to the other side of the open doorway just to be safe, thankful that the ancient floor didn't creak under her weight and the suddenness of her move.

"Maybe you'd prefer that I call you Blue."

She tensed. He hadn't given her a straightforward answer, but he'd narrowed the possibilities. Besides her family, only her close friends and the people with whom she worked knew the nickname she'd been called all her life—bestowed because of the unusual deep color of her eyes.

She'd told Lowell. This had to be Drake. Or someone he'd hired to scare her off.

"I asked you to identify yourself," she demanded, impatience and anger searing away any lingering fear. If this guy was yanking her around—

"I'm the man you came all this way to protect." He laughed softly, the sound shivering across her frazzled nerve endings. "Ironic, isn't it?"

She shook off the effect his voice had on her and issued yet another demand. "Prove it. Show yourself."

She didn't know how much he'd changed in the past five years or what physical scars he'd suffered, but she would surely recognize him to a degree from the picture in the mission profile. The Noah Drake of five years ago had thick, dark hair and even darker brown eyes. He'd been a hell of a good-looking guy with an athletic body to match.

But that had all likely changed.

"You'll just have to trust me," he said, that smooth voice containing a challenge now. "Besides, I don't think you want to risk further exposure to the curse."

Curse? She wanted to throttle whoever he was. "Just show yourself or some ID and everything will be cool," she told him flatly. No way was she stepping out into the open until she knew who this guy was. *Curse.* Yeah, right.

"There's a small cemetery behind this old chapel," he went on as if she hadn't said a word. "They say there's a voodoo witch buried there and anyone who comes near her grave will die a terrible death. Now you don't want that, do you, *Specialist* Callahan?"

It *was* Drake. He had the kind of high-level clearance to know the organization that had actually sent her. Lowell only knew that Rothman had hired her. She kept to herself the litany of adjectives that tumbled into her mind. Very descriptive adjectives she was certain Drake wouldn't want to hear since they all accurately expressed what she thought about him at the moment.

"I'm not afraid of any curse." Blue stepped out into the open, but didn't put her gun away. She turned slowly, peering into the darkness for any manifestation of Drake. "Nor am I the one receiving the death threats."

"No one has actually threatened my life," he argued pointedly and without conviction.

Blue whipped in the direction of the sound, it was closer and from her left this time. Where the hell was he?

"Then why am I here?" she argued. "And why are you being so secretive? Why didn't you call out to me when I was running like hell through these damned woods?" She was mad now.

"Hmm." The sound seemed to resonate all around her. She trembled in spite of the anger fueling her courage. "First," the taunting words went on, "you're here because Edgar Rothman feels guilty." Pause. "Secondly, I didn't call out to you until I was sure."

Drake was right behind her.

Blue spun around. "Sure of what?"

She blinked. Nothing. Only darkness.

"That there was no one else except you."

"Where the hell are you?" This had gone far enough.

"Turn around, Specialist Callahan," he said as if she were a child, "and walk straight ahead. You'll find the house in that direction."

"Why can't I see you?" Frustration made her voice tight and a little high-pitched. She did as he said and turned around slowly, very slowly, but she didn't like this one bit.

"Straight ahead, Blue," he ordered.

She stiffened her spine and tightened her grip on her weapon. Whatever his game, she wasn't playing. Maybe Rothman didn't know his friend had dropped over the edge, but he was going to find out the minute Blue got back to a phone. "I'm not going anywhere until you tell me why I can't see you."

"Then it's going to be a long night for you, I fear."

He was gone.

Though she hadn't heard a sound and damned sure hadn't seen him, she knew it as surely as she knew her own name. The air felt suddenly thinner, lighter, as if a presence that diminished all else had abruptly vanished.

Blue shook herself. Maybe the intensity was just her imagination. With the silence coagulating around her, she was beginning to think she'd imagined the whole conversation. This was too damned strange.

Deciding not to take the word of some disembodied voice, she moved slowly around the old building he'd called a chapel and looked for a path of any sort leading away from it. The moon's light was scarcely any help, but she was glad for it. She stumbled again, this time over a rock. She straightened and glared down at the hindrance in her path.

It wasn't a rock.

An old headstone stared back at her.

MAGGIE "BLUE" CALLAHAN made her way back to the house much more quickly than Noah had anticipated. She had more guts than he'd given her credit for. He'd stayed close the entire journey just in case. Though she hadn't heard him and definitely hadn't seen him, she'd known, or at least suspected, that he was there. She'd stopped and looked directly at him twice. Her perceptiveness was uncanny.

Noah smiled. Unexpected. He enjoyed that aspect of observing her, even if her presence did infuriate him.

He'd watched her on the beach. She didn't look like a bodyguard. Not only was she female, but she was attractive as well. Long blond hair that she didn't bother to restrain had drifted over her shoulders and danced playfully at the wind's invitation. She stood tall and slender, but she didn't look thin. Rather she appeared fit and strong. But it was the curve of her cheek and the masterfully carved details of her mouth that had held his attention the longest.

Very attractive. Also unexpected.

She'd felt him watching her even then.

The technology that allowed him to view the world in any capacity during daylight hours was best described as high-powered sunglasses or the reverse of night vision, all built into a savvy camera with zoom and wide-angle capabilities. In his room, as in the main parlor, there was a monitor which he could tune to east, west, north or south, and see all angles from the house. This was his only means of self-protection during the day, other than Lowell's presence. Well, there was the escape tunnel...but that was a last resort. Only he knew of its existence and it held dangers of its own.

She'd walked along that beach, staring out over his ocean as the sun dipped beneath the horizon and he'd grown aroused by the image. He'd longed to taste the length of her slender throat...those lush lips. To trace her body with his hands.

He forced away the frustrating thoughts. For five long years he had disciplined himself against all emotion, all needs that didn't equate to survival. He would not allow this woman to shake what he'd suffered endless hours, days and months to build.

Blue was at the front door again, unlocking it with trembling fingers. He heard her muttered curses as she tried twice to accomplish her task. Noah moved to the rear of the house where he would prepare before going inside for their first and only face-to-face meeting.

No matter how efficient or attractive Miss Callahan was, he didn't want her here.

He didn't need anyone else.

And he definitely couldn't risk losing control. Firm, relentless control was all that got him through each day.

"I said, I want to see Mr. Drake."

The sound of Blue's outrage carried through the house and was now directed at Lowell. She'd stormed into the kitchen and demanded to know where Noah was. Lowell, of course, had no idea.

"I'm sorry, I'm not sure where he is at the moment." He raised his empty palms, but even that seemingly nonchalant gesture didn't hide his mounting concern. "When he heard the shots," Lowell explained, "he rushed out. He hasn't come back."

Blue's furious expression didn't change. "Does he keep any weapons on the premises?" She glared at Lowell, daring him to avoid the truth. "Say a high-powered rifle, maybe?"

Noah smiled, amused once more by her fierce determination. So she thought he'd been the one doing the shooting to scare her off. Oh, he wanted rid of her right enough, but he wouldn't go to that extreme.

"What are you suggesting?" Lowell demanded, affronted. He was a loyal friend, even if Noah was loath to admit it.

"I'm suggesting—"

"Good evening, Miss Callahan," Noah said as he strode into the kitchen before she took her interrogation tactics further. Blue Callahan didn't give up easily. That had quickly become clear as he'd hesitated, listening, in the small hall that separated the kitchen from the screened porch.

Startled, her intense glower shifted to him. She blinked rapidly as if caught off guard by what she saw. He had no idea what she'd expected.

"The answer to your question is yes." He moved across the room, stopping only when he was close enough to attempt to intimidate her with his presence. She was tall, but several inches shorter than he was.

And he was stronger. Though he doubted he would garner much success at bullying her physically. She looked more than capable of holding her own. "I have several weapons at my disposal and you're welcome to inspect them all. They are presently locked in a gun cabinet upstairs."

Blue wasn't intimidated, startled maybe, but not afraid in the least. He almost smiled as respect bloomed inside him. She appraised him thoroughly, taking her sweet time. He tensed beneath that level of scrutiny. He couldn't remember the last time he'd been looked at so long and carefully by anyone, much less a woman.

Now he was the one intimidated. It was almost laughable. But Noah wasn't laughing.

"Mr. Drake, I presume?" she said pointedly when at last she'd completed her visual examination. He didn't miss the flicker of approval amidst the fury in those extraordinary eyes.

He realized now why she was nicknamed Blue. The zoom and detail-distinction capabilities of his equipment weren't quite good enough to provide the finer details. Her eyes were incredible. The most intense shade of blue he'd ever seen. He wondered if the hue would be as dark when she wasn't quite so angry.

"You might as well know up front that I don't want you here," he said in lieu of acknowledging his identity and forcing away the dangerous thoughts his mind insisted on conjuring. "Since it would be next to impossible to get a boat to take you back to the mainland at this time of the evening, you're welcome to stay the night." He pressed her with a look he felt certain spoke volumes about his irrevocable stand on the matter. "But first thing tomorrow morning you will leave this property."

She didn't waver in the slightest. "It doesn't matter that someone was shooting—"

"At you," he pointed out. "It could have been one of the locals who despises outlanders. Or an unscrupulous hunter who failed to consider where his stray shots might end up."

She rolled her eyes and shook her head, impatience radiating off her in waves. "Yeah, right. You know that isn't the case. I know when I'm being shot at."

"Whatever the case," he said without hesitation or further consideration. "Tomorrow morning you will leave. Goodnight, Maggie Callahan." He strode across the room without looking at her. He didn't need her here. The only thing he needed was to be left alone.

"Don't get your hopes up."

The sound of her defiance brought him up short.

He turned around slowly, leveled his gaze on her extraordinary blue one. "What did you say?"

Arms folded over her chest, she strolled up to him and looked him square in the eyes. "I said," she repeated pointedly, "don't get your hopes up. I have an assignment."

She poked him in the chest with her forefinger. He frowned, unaccustomed to human touch after all this time.

"You're that assignment. I have a problem with failure." She smiled up at him, the gesture lacking humor but underscoring her determination perfectly. "Good night, Noah Drake."

She walked out of the room without a backward glance.

Chapter Four

Blue spent her first night and full day on St. Gabriel Island learning the area around Drake's home and developing a routine. The security on the island was nonexistent. Anyone could dock almost anywhere and come ashore without notice. According to Lowell there were scarcely more than a few hundred residents and some of those were only part-timers. A couple of the summer homes often sat empty the entire season, offering the perfect refuge for any sort of unsavory characters.

Chester, the self-appointed lookout for the islanders, spent the better part of his days strolling about and monitoring the goings-on here and there. So far, he had noted nothing out of the ordinary except that one of Widow Paisley's cats had gone missing. He was sure the animal, being a tomcat, would show up in a day or two.

Blue had given Lowell a panic pager. It was smaller than a disposable lighter and could be easily kept in his trouser pocket. Any time she was out of sight and he needed her, all he had to do was depress the button and her pager would go off, alerting her to his distress. She hoped Drake would carry one as well, but she doubted his cooperation on any level, much less one that indicated his need to have her around. According to Lowell, he even refused to use the security system installed years ago in the house. It wasn't top of the line, but it was there.

She glanced at the darkening sky as she moved around the perimeter of the yard, careful to stay within the concealing fringes of the trees. Five minutes tops and it would be completely dark and she would be inside. She shivered as the low-lying fog rolled in around her. It was truly creepy. Lowell had warned her that the rare cool summer night often invited the fog. It floated on the air like wispy ghosts. It made the ordinary look alien. Between the eerie mist and the smell—the ancient, seagully odor that worked deep into her nose and awakened some rarely used area of gray matter that was perfectly capable of believing in monsters—she was edgier than usual.

Considering Drake's nocturnal habits and the need for daytime observations, she had opted to sleep in increments, a few minutes here and a few there. She'd learned that little exercise in discipline from her fellow Specialists, Ferrelli and Logan, who had gained the skill while in the military.

The ability to drop immediately to sleep and grab forty winks whenever possible was immensely helpful when she needed to be available 24/7. Bad guys didn't keep bankers' hours, nor did she have the personnel at hand to rotate shifts. She was lucky Drake had permitted her to stay. Lowell was livid at his continued insistence that he didn't need anyone. Bottom line: she was it. Lucas would be nearby, but only as backup. His presence would not be given away unless absolutely necessary.

Noah Drake did not want her here in any capacity. Blue had a hunch about that persistent attitude. The man wasn't stupid by any stretch of the imagination. She had a growing suspicion that he no longer cared…that he wanted to face whatever lay in store for him and get it over with. Maybe he was simply tired of living the way he did.

Sympathy shouldered its way to the forefront of her emotions. "Dammit," she muttered. She did not want to feel sympathetic toward the man. He would pick up on that line of thinking immediately and his reaction would not be pleasant. He had certainly done nothing to garner sympathy or any other softer emotion from her, but she wasn't stupid either. He had suffered greatly…still suffered. Whatever he had done for his government had altered his life to a significant degree. How could the man have any kind of social life? Career? Or anything else? He couldn't. Not really. Any friend or lover would be forced to live in darkness just as he did.

Blue muttered another curse. Just what she needed…tender feelings for the guy. He was a class-A jerk. Yes, admittedly, it was too bad that his life pretty much sucked, but did he have to be mean-spirited to those who tried to help him?

She stilled, the mist swirling around her like curling tentacles, but she scarcely noticed. Yes. He did have to be indifferent…condescending…and flat-out mean. It was the only way to prevent bonding. Becoming attached to anyone, male or female, could be costly. Noah Drake could not depend on another human being freely choosing his way of life. No matter how enamored a woman might become of him—and Blue could definitely see that happening—she would resent a nocturnal existence as soon as the novelty wore off.

Oh, Noah Drake would definitely have no difficulty attracting the opposite sex. He was incredibly good-looking, well-built, and there was something about his eyes. Something that went well beyond the size, shape and color...something magnetic, hypnotic. Then there was that square, chiseled jaw and strong chin that always looked shadowed with his dark coloring. And that mouth was no common feature either. It was full, masterfully sculpted and undeniably sensual.

She moistened her lips and released a long, slow breath. She would *not* be physically attracted to him. That was not only a major professional no-no, it was a personal disaster. Her career was her life...Noah Drake resented the very government she deeply respected.

The adage "as different as night and day" precisely described the two of them in far more ways than one.

Blue slipped onto the screened back porch and glanced one last time at the sun as it sank beneath the horizon, dragging the few remaining veins of gold and orange from the marbled ebony sky. Soon Noah Drake would rise to greet the night.

Awareness quivered through her, but she squashed the sensation. This was business...nothing more.

Stepping into the kitchen, she inhaled deeply. A sweet and tangy exotic scent tantalized her senses, making her mouth water. "Mercy, Lowell," she almost moaned. "I hope that's on tonight's menu."

He glanced up from the stove. "It's my own special Asian chicken recipe. I hope you'll like it."

Blue moved closer to the stove and peered into the large wok. Red and green peppers, scallions, snow peas and even pineapple were sautèing in a dark liquid along with slender strips of chicken.

"Mmm...looks wonderful."

Lowell winked. For an older guy he was a bit of a flirt. "It is, trust me."

Though she certainly didn't want to encourage him, she couldn't help but smile. Lowell Kline was incorrigible. She hitched a thumb towards the second floor. "Gotta shower, but I'll be right back."

A frown furrowed across his brow. "Before you go," he said hesitantly, "you should know that Chester phoned while you were out."

"Really?" She forced her brain to focus on the conversation rather than the delicious aroma of the concoction in the wok. "Did the Widow Paisley find her cat?" she suggested teasingly.

A smile replaced Lowell's frown. "Yes, but that's not why Chester called. He ran into a couple of men, outlanders, at BullDog's last night."

Blue's interest piqued. "Did he give you a description or other pertinent details?"

Lowell nodded. "He said the two were young, rather rakish-looking and were bragging about playing target practice with unsuspecting *human* targets."

Blue doubted *rakish* was in Chester's vocabulary, but she got the idea. "He thinks they were the ones who shot at me yesterday?"

Another succinct nod. "One of them said something about scaring a blonde and hoping to run across her again. Chester is certain he was referring to you. I told him not to worry—that Mr. Drake said you were a fighter."

She tried not to put too much stock in Drake's comment. Instead she considered Chester's report. The

likelihood that the real threat to Noah Drake would
hang out in a place like BullDog's and brag about his
exploits was about zero. Maybe the bullets she'd
dodged yesterday were fired by a couple of cognitively
delinquent punks, but it just didn't feel right. Blue had
been shot at enough times to know what real intent
felt like.

"Do you think you should call your friend Lucas
Camp and have him send someone to check it out? He
might even want to come himself."

Blue shook her head. "Not just yet. That's really
more a matter for the local authorities. Maybe Chester
should report the incident to the sheriff."

Lowell turned the gas off beneath the wok and
placed a lid over it to allow the contents to steam amid
the fragrant sauce. Blue's senses as well as her stomach lodged a protest at being denied the pleasure of
the aroma.

"Chester did say that he planned to inform the authorities," Lowell went on. "But his real concern was
for your and Mr. Drake's safety since the hoodlums
are still loitering about. The sheriff might not get
around to looking into the problem for a day or two.
Sometimes, here on the island, we're forced to take
care of things on our own." He looked thoughtful for
a moment. "Chester did say that he hopes to locate
where the two are hanging out and pass that information along to the authorities as well."

Blue didn't like the sound of that. "If Chester starts
following those guys around, he might be the one in
danger," she said, automatically worrying about the
old guy. Not only was he a good connection to the
residents here that she didn't want to lose, she genu-
inely liked him. Unlike Noah Drake, Blue formed at-

tachments quickly. She hoped that wasn't one character trait she'd come to regret...especially where he was concerned.

Lowell set another pan atop the stove. Blue's gaze followed his movements, wondering vaguely what delight he planned next.

"Chester can take care of himself," he assured her. "Don't bother worrying about him. You shouldn't be fooled by his laid-back manner, he's as cagey as they come."

Blue shrugged. "It's a habit with me. I grew up in a house with five brothers. I know how much trouble guys can get into." When Lowell lifted a skeptical eyebrow, she adopted an immediate expression of contrition. "Present company excluded, of course."

"Five brothers." He shook his head in wonder. "My, your poor mother must've had her hands full."

Blue laughed softly remembering the day the youngest of her brothers graduated from the police academy. Her mother had said a prayer of thanks that God had gotten her last son through to manhood, then she'd crossed herself and added that she hoped all would go well from there. Men were such babies. She'd heard her mother say it a thousand times.

And it was true—at times—of all men.

She wondered if Drake ever suffered one of those petulant moments. She almost shook her head at the thought. No, he would never allow such a lapse in control. She suddenly wished he would. For just one minute she'd love to see him totally out of control.

"...they were all I had."

Blue snapped back to attention. "I'm sorry. What were you saying?" She'd zoned out completely there for a moment.

Lowell looked startled, as if he'd just realized that he'd spoken aloud. "My family," he said quickly. "I lost them…"

She couldn't imagine the emptiness of being completely alone in the world. "Your whole family? That's terrible."

He looked away, the pan on the stove forgotten for the moment. "Yes."

His sadness was palpable. "Some sort of accident?" She asked before she thought.

Lowell's gaze settled heavily onto hers. "Murdered."

The announcement startled her…or maybe it was the tone he used. Fierce…pointed. Lowell Kline had obviously not gotten over the loss. She could certainly understand how difficult it would be to try and get past that kind of tragedy.

She touched his arm reassuringly. "I hope the person responsible is paying dearly for his actions."

Lowell's expression hardened, but a knowing smirk tilted his lips. "They've paid all right," he said. "More than even they know."

Her tension elevated. But, Blue considered, the loss of an entire family to violence would likely evoke this kind of intense reaction in the remaining family member. Maybe he didn't like to talk about it.

Lowell seemed suddenly to realize he'd startled her. "You'll have to forgive me," he said with obvious remorse. "My family is a sore subject for me."

She patted him on the arm once more. "I understand. I can't imagine losing even one of my brothers."

Glancing toward the ceiling, Lowell said, "I wonder what's keeping Mr. Drake? He's usually up by now."

The notion that Drake might have risen already and left by the front door to prevent having to deal with Blue slammed into her midsection with all the force of a physical blow.

"I think I'll head on up for that shower now."

His attention returning to the stovetop, Lowell reminded her, "Dinner should be ready in ten minutes."

"Can't wait," she called over her shoulder, refraining from breaking into a run as she left the room.

If Noah Drake had left the house without informing her, she was going to...

She took the stairs two at a time. Well, she didn't know what she was going to do. But whatever it was, he wasn't going to like it.

Her pace increased as she moved down the second-floor hall. Lowell had warned her that the third floor was off limits, and she hadn't had a problem with that...until now.

She had a job to do and Noah was going to have to start cooperating at least a little. Blue Callahan wouldn't lose her first principal as a Specialist because he was too hardheaded to listen to reason.

Standing at the bottom of the smaller staircase that led to the third floor, she took a moment to catch her breath...to bolster her courage actually. He wasn't going to like this if he was still up there. She thought about him wandering in the dark with two trigger-happy bozos running around. He might not like her trespassing into his private male domain but...

"Too bad," she murmured.

She moved up the stairs, taking care not to make a sound. On the small landing there was only one door...*his*. She started to knock, but the small crack between the door and the frame stopped her. She swore hotly, repeatedly, under her breath. The door wasn't closed all the way. Lowell had told her that Drake kept his door closed and locked at all times when he was in his room.

Drake was gone.

She started to turn away, but then thought better of it. She might not get a chance to check out his room again. What the heck? She was here. Might as well make the most of the opportunity. That would teach him to run out on her.

Holding her breath, she pushed the door inward. Thank God it didn't creak. Like the rest of the house the room was pretty damned dark, but she was getting used to it little by little. A sitting area greeted her as she stepped inside the room. There was a television and an extensive collection of electronics for listening to music and playing DVDs. An open laptop computer sat on a desk on the far side of the sitting area, the screen saver sending dim bands of light dancing across the room. She moved farther into the room and noted three doors. Two were typical interior doors, most likely to the bathroom and closet. The third was bolted shut with a total of six deadbolt locks. She frowned, wondering where it led—then it hit her. The widow's walk.

She looked to her left where a wall of windows looked out over the ocean, but heavy draperies blocked the lovely view. Behind the drapes she knew there would be closed hurricane shutters beyond the glass. The carpeting was dark, red maybe, like that on the stairs. A massive armoire stood against the wall next to the heavily bolted door. When she reached the middle of the room, she turned around slowly, taking in the whole picture.

The furnishings were either antique or perfect reproductions. There were no photographs or artwork on the walls. A few books were scattered on the table near the small sofa. She considered checking the titles but forgot all about the books as her gaze moved over the bed. Large. Four-poster. The linens were rumpled. Drawn like smoke to fire, she moved closer. Her mind conjured the darkly handsome image of Noah lying amid those tousled sheets. She closed her eyes and inhaled deeply, the slightest hint of his male scent still lingered there. Heat and a new kind of hunger stirred deep inside her.

She opened her eyes and studied the pillow and the impression that still marred it. Instinctively she reached out and touched the place where he had lain. Something electrical passed through her and she shivered. The bed wasn't even cold yet. He hadn't been gone long.

Another flash of fury sent those other foolish sensations scurrying for parts unknown.

It was time she and Noah Drake had a serious talk.

One of the doors on the other side of the room suddenly opened.

Blue's gaze swiveled in that direction. Her heart surged into her throat...then stopped altogether.

Noah Drake stood in the doorway that no doubt led to the en suite bathroom, naked save for a towel slung carelessly around his lean hips.

"What are you doing in here?"

The rich, deep sound of that voice, even filled with anger and accusation, affected her in a way that was beyond her control.

"I thought you'd run out on me again." She swallowed tightly and realized then and there how lame her excuse sounded. But it was true and she'd taken the opportunity to snoop. Now she was caught. "I came up to check...and the door was open so I assumed..."

He moved in her direction. "You assumed I was out, giving you the perfect occasion to nose around." The accusation was stinging. As he came closer she could see the tightness of his features, the barely restrained fury. He was madder than hell and close to taking it out on her in more ways than maybe she was prepared to deal with.

"Yes," she admitted, mainly because one word was about all she could manage. With him less than two feet away, she could see the water droplets still clinging to his olive skin and the smoothness of his freshly shaven jaw. He'd missed a smidgen of shaving lather. She resisted the urge to reach up and wipe it away. His hair was still wet, looking exactly as if he'd done no more than run his fingers through it to push it out of his way.

He shifted that dark, hypnotic gaze from her to his bed and back. Heat exploded inside her, sending stream after stream of hot, urgent sensations through her body. She trembled once before she conquered the weakness, but her heart rate would not slow, her rapid intake of breath belied her composure.

"What did you expect? A coffin maybe? Or did you expect more of a laboratory setting? The kind of place you see in the old Frankenstein movies?"

She shook her head. "I didn't expect anything like that...I—"

"My private space is off limits, Miss Callahan." He moved closer still...until she could smell the freshly showered scent of his skin and the male essence that was his exclusively. She tried not to look…that was the last thing she needed, but she just couldn't help herself. He was too gorgeous…too splendid to ignore. His skin was smooth, sprinkled lightly with dark hair. But it was the exquisite muscle definition that played utter havoc with her brain.

Whatever had happened to him five years ago, there was no outward indication that he was anything other than perfect.

"I…I'm sorry," she finally managed, dragging her gaze up to his. This proved even more unsettling. Even in the low light, it was impossible to miss the sexual hunger glittering behind all that anger in those deep-brown eyes.

This was not good.

"I should give you some privacy to…to…" she blurted, stalled, then swallowed. She had to pull it back together. Calm…cool…collected. "I apologize, but I only came up here because I was concerned about you. It *is* my job."

Beneath that fierce, penetrating gaze, she felt suddenly and utterly naked. Despite the button-down blouse worn over a tank top, the jeans and two loaded weapons, she felt completely disarmed, bare. Maybe if the blouse and jeans had been more loosely fitting or if she'd buttoned the blouse all the way to her neck…maybe then she wouldn't be feeling quite so exposed.

As it was, that gaze roamed over her like an exploring caress. Over the bare skin at her throat and in the V of her blouse. Down her arms, unshielded by the sleeveless blouse. Then over her denim-clad legs. More of those little bursts of heat flared inside her. She'd never once considered her manner of dress as anything other than utilitarian, functional. But now, she felt exposed…uncovered.

She curled her fingers into fists, fastened her gaze on the door, and forced herself to put one foot in front of the other. A smart person knew the time to make an exit. When she would have moved past him, he encircled her arm with those long, strong fingers. He restrained her for three long beats before speaking. Then, he looked down his shoulder and directly into her eyes.

"I don't think you realize just how dangerous it is here for you."

His tone was thick with desire and promise, soft in a way that was lethal to all that made her woman. Her breath evaporated in her lungs as she lifted her gaze to his. There was no mistaking what she saw there. The intensity of his sexuality…his hunger made her tremble in spite of her best efforts to keep the outward response in check.

"I've been in dangerous situations before," she said, her voice almost as husky as his. "I'm not afraid of risking my life for a client. It's what I do."

He watched intently as she spoke, followed every movement of her lips, then shifted that dark, dark gaze back to hers. "There's a great deal more here to fear than physical danger from my enemies, Maggie Callahan. Are you sure you're prepared to stay?"

Her attention drifted down to that awesome chest…and lower to where white terry cloth draped loosely around lean hips, then up again…back to those devastatingly hypnotic eyes. "I've never been more sure of anything in my life." She smiled when surprise flared in those dark depths. "You won't scare me off so easily, *Noah Drake*," she added, emphasizing his name with a sultry inflection that surprised even her. "I always did love a challenge."

He released her as abruptly as he'd taken hold of her. "Don't ever come up here again." There was nothing soft about his voice this time. Anger glittered in his eyes now. His ploy hadn't worked, and he was mad as hell about it.

Victory drew her lips into a smile. "Noted," she acknowledged the order and walked away without a backward glance.

Once on the landing outside his door she closed her eyes and drew in a deep, bolstering breath.

That was too close for comfort. She inventoried her body's infernal reaction to the man and cursed herself. She had to find a way to ignore him on that level.

She almost laughed out loud at the foolishness of that proposal as she slowly descended the stairs. Ignoring her responses to him would be about as easy as keeping the sun from rising.

Chapter Five

Noah sat alone at his desk downstairs and methodically reviewed all but one piece of the day's mail. Tension vibrated inside him. He shoved his chair back from the desk and pushed to his feet. Damn his lack of control.

Lowell and Blue were having dinner. He had refused to dine with them. And still he could not block *her* from his thoughts. Like the woman, the idea of her simply refused to vacate his mind. He cursed his uncharacteristic weakness.

He moved across the room…stood at the wide set of windows and closed his eyes, summoning the ocean view beyond the heavily shrouded sashes of glass. The dense woods, veiled in darkness now. The full moon hanging low overhead, spilling a dim glow over all that lay beneath it. The smell of the Atlantic…the night sounds of the tide…of the leaves swaying in the gentle breeze. The weather forecaster had promised unseasonably cool temperatures tonight, there would be mist in the air, cloud-like forms floating like whispers from the past. He yearned to touch the night…to feel it around him.

But he was no longer alone in his misery.

She would follow him if he left the house.

Never had he met such a determined woman. He opened his eyes and stared at nothing at all. He'd been certain that if his indifference didn't push her away, the threat of physical intimacy would.

It had not.

She was not afraid of him on any level.

He shook his head slowly from side to side.

She had to have a weakness. Everyone had one. He had to find it…and then he would be the one in control.

The scope of his world had been narrowed so much that he felt completely out of sorts if even one aspect was beyond his dominion. She threw him off balance…threatened his ability to maintain absolute authority over all, meager as it was, that his world encompassed.

He knew a great deal about Maggie "Blue" Callahan, at least as much as was recorded by her employer. The youngest in a family composed mostly of males, she had strived to make her own mark. She'd done that and more. Noah couldn't help wondering if the former president had been enthralled with her outstanding abilities as a personal protector or with the woman herself. Though he did not doubt her capabilities, Noah's money was on the latter.

Beauty went only skin deep, and she was beautiful and more. The perfect mix of femininity and athleticism made her slender form unforgettable. Long, silky blond hair and heart-stopping blue eyes embellished a face that was an incredible blend of softness and angularity. Being smart and determined only made bad matters worse. But it was the genuine compassion, the burning desire to succeed beneath all the appealing outer trappings that distracted him the most.

He never doubted for one moment her ability to hold her own in a physical confrontation. He'd seen firsthand her agility and the sharpness of her instincts. She was good. At twenty-eight, he wondered if she had a serious relationship in D.C. or back home in California. He didn't want to wonder, but he couldn't help himself.

She intrigued him as no one else ever had.

That glitch was dangerous to both of them.

General Bonner wanted him dead...wanted vengeance. He would stop at nothing to have it, Noah was certain. That put Blue directly in the line of fire. But then, she was trained for that precise position. Be that as it may, he had a bad feeling that nothing had prepared her for this unexpected attraction. He was no fool. She felt it the same as he did.

Basic chemistry, he understood that. But there were times when even the most elemental chemistry could be volatile. This was one of the times.

His loins tightened at the mere thought of touching her.

"You ruined Lowell's evening, you know."

The sound of her voice dragged his reluctant attention around to the other side of the room. She stood in the doorway looking annoyed and impatient. He suddenly wondered how a simple pair of off-the-rack blue denim jeans could mold so perfectly to the human form. How a rather nondescript navy blouse that buttoned down the front, could look so utterly feminine and tailor-made to fit her torso? There was no reasonable explanation for the direction of his thoughts other than the fact that he had not touched a woman in five long years. And this one was here—right in front of him—vibrant and attractive, determined to barge into his life at his every turn.

She moved toward him, her head inclined, studying him as if she could read his thoughts. "Dinner was fabulous. You do have to eat."

His body tensed as she surveyed him from head to toe. He wore what he always did, black jeans and a black T-shirt. His closet contained nothing else. But she looked at him as if seeing him for the first time…as if taking his measure. The breadth of his shoulders. His fingers curled into fists as her gaze moved over his torso, paused strategically, then moved down the length of his legs.

She continued moving toward him until she was only a few feet away. Her gaze returned to his, approval glimmered there. "You look healthy enough, but I'd like you to stay that way…at least while you're under my watch."

It was at that exact moment that Noah knew beyond a shadow of a doubt just how much of a threat she represented to his hard-won peace with himself.

Five endless years it had taken him to find this elusive plateau…this place where he could survive above the bitterness and anger and without looking back and wondering what might have been had he made different choices. He'd even found an outlet for his need to accomplish something. Now, in barely twenty-four hours, she had shaken the foundation of all he was. All it had taken was a look, a touch…the sound of her voice.

"I'm not a child, Maggie Callahan. I know when to eat."

He didn't miss the slight tightening of her jaw. She

didn't like it that he referred to her that way. She wanted him to accept her presence and call her Blue as her friends did, but he would not. He would use whatever means available to maintain the distance between them until he discovered a weakness of hers that would put him back in control.

"If you're planning a stroll, I'd appreciate it if you let me know. I need to be aware of your location at all times." She folded her arms over her chest and dared him to argue with her order.

He considered the weapon strapped to her shoulder. "Your protection is not required during the night hours." He leveled his most intimidating gaze on her. "No one can touch me in the dark."

Memories of the moments they'd spent together near the old chapel last night tumbled through her head. He didn't have to be a mind reader to know, the slight widening of her eyes, the catch in her breath gave her thoughts away.

She lifted her chin a notch and glared at him defiantly. "So, you're at home in the dark. That's great. But it changes nothing. Where you go, I go."

He nodded once, conceding the point. It would be in his best interest to keep her close by. There was only one way to determine a person's weaknesses and that was to acquaint oneself well with that person. Five years ago he would not have considered the job a hardship. Things were different now, and he recognized the risk involved. He didn't want to know her *that* well. He didn't want her here at all.

Well, *want* actually had nothing to do with it.

If he could not intimidate her into leaving, then he would make the situation work to his advantage. The past five years had taught him one thing if nothing else, he could learn to live with anything if he set his mind to it.

"I received another letter today," he said offhandedly.

The announcement took her by surprise. "Where is it? I'd like to see it."

She followed him to his desk where the white envelope lay untouched. He'd recognized it immediately and set it to the side. He'd first considered throwing it away. If no more letters were reported then perhaps Rothman would see the uselessness of having her here. But then he'd decided against that course of action. Though he resented the intrusion of her presence, he resented being stalked even more. Bonner clearly knew Noah's every move, but this pointless game was so unlike him.

Callahan opened the envelope and unfolded the single page inside. She looked at it for a long, assessing minute, then passed it to him.

I'm closer than you know. She won't be able to stop me.

Just as he had suspected, she was in the direct line of fire from whatever source this threat came. "You understand that you will be a primary target now?" he asked her, his gaze searching hers. He needed to know that she understood fully the ramifications of her continued presence in this house.

"I understand. I understood it yesterday when those punks took shots at me."

He frowned. "What punks?"

She quickly gave him an update on Chester's findings in regard to the gunshots.

Anger infused Noah. This was not the general's

style at all. This incident was exactly what it had appeared—two fools with too much time on their hands.

There was only one way to deal with a fool.

"I'm going out," he announced. "Now."

He didn't give her time to argue or question his agenda. He simply walked out.

She followed.

"Should I hold dinner for you?" Lowell asked as Noah passed through the kitchen.

"I can fend for myself later," he answered without slowing. This was his home...his refuge. He would not be threatened for no reason in his own home.

He and General Bonner had a score to settle. Not that Noah thought Bonner was right in any sense of the word. But at least he had credible motivation for his actions.

Fury washed over Noah anew.

Two punks using Callahan for target practice was unacceptable.

The moment he was outside he lingered for a time to draw in a deep breath of fresh night air. As predicted, the temperature was cool...mist drifted through the darkness, the moonlight doing nothing to banish it.

The frothy water lapped at the sand, teasing, twirling, then draining away. Noah moved toward it, the sound like a beacon in the darkness. He loved the ocean. That it rolled across the sand of his own backyard made him feel very lucky indeed. This was his one pleasure...his one escape.

As long as he had this he could survive the long nights spent alone.

"It's so beautiful here."

He turned sharply toward her, having almost forgotten she was there. The sparse moonbeams, captured the gold in her honey-colored hair, making it gleam like raw silk. Her full attention was riveted to the waves crashing against the sand, the sound as well as the sight mesmerizing.

She looked up at him then. "This is why you chose this place, isn't it?"

For a time he stood there, his gaze connected with hers in a long, evocative stare, without responding to her question. Then he said, "Yes."

Her gaze shifted back to the restless water. "I can see why."

He wanted to touch her. Wanted to feel her lips beneath his. But that would be a mistake.

Instead, he strode toward the forest and the refuge it offered. He could lose himself in there. Watch for intruders while clearing his mind of notions that could not be seen to fruition.

She stayed right behind him for a time and then he did what he did best now, he disappeared into the darkness.

Blue searched for at least half an hour. Had she not gotten such a good lay of the land today, she would be unequivocally lost right now.

Noah Drake, however, was lost to her. He disappeared into the night like a shadow…like a part of it. She heard not one sound, saw not the first hint of movement. He made her madder than hell.

How was she supposed to keep him safe if he vanished on her? Not only did it prevent her from doing her job, his little disappearing acts made her look totally inept. Then again, she imagined that was part of the reason he did it. He wanted her to feel inadequate…to prove he didn't need her.

Well, he was making his point.

A little too well.

She considered that the yahoos with the target-practice fetish could be out here in the dark somewhere and that made her uneasy. But then again, if she couldn't find Drake, chances were those guys couldn't either.

The idea that he might be lurking about watching her made her want to kick his...

Movement to her right.

Blue turned slowly, careful not to make a sound and squinted into the darkness. A shaft of moonlight penetrated the canopy of trees about five yards away. She unholstered her weapon and took a bead in the direction of the next sound. A figure stepped into the light.

"Strange things happening round here," a female voice said, the sound coarse with age.

An old woman, short and stocky, stood in that minuscule cone of light, her mahogany skin weathered, making her look even older than Blue first estimated. She wore her hair back in some kind of bandanna. She dressed plainly except for the layers of odd-looking jewelry, and was clearly unarmed, though she appeared completely unafraid in spite of the bead Blue had on her. But the most prominent feature about her was the scar that slashed from the edge of her right eye to the corner of her mouth. The whiteness of it stood out in stark relief against her dark skin.

Lowering her weapon only slightly, Blue moved closer. "Who are you?" Goose bumps skittered across her skin. She tried to shake off a ridiculous feeling. She wasn't afraid of any old woman...but some instinct warned her to beware.

"Makes no nevermind who I am," the woman returned pointedly. "But you, now there's a horse of a different color. You're in way over your head. There's something bad coming. If you're not mighty careful the darkness will get you. You're right to be afraid."

Against her own better judgment, Blue lowered her weapon the rest of the way. Something about the woman rattled Blue, made her uneasy. "Who are you?" she repeated. And how the hell did she know Blue was afraid of the dark?

"You mind my words, *Maggie Callahan*," the old woman said. "Things are not always what they seem."

"How do you know my name?" Blue's heart pounded against her sternum. "Tell me who—"

It was too late. She was gone.

The old woman simply melted into the darkness the same way Drake seemed to do.

Blue scrubbed a hand over her face and reached for calm. She was shaking. She cursed herself under her breath. It was a small island. Probably all the residents knew about her by now. Chester's doing, she would just bet. She was overreacting, that's all. The old woman was only trying to spook her.

Blue's eyes narrowed. The idea that Drake may have put the old woman up to this sent anger whipping along every raw nerve ending. When she found him again, she was going to let him have it, with both barrels, so to speak.

She shoved her weapon back into its holster and decided to make her way to the old chapel. She had a sneaking suspicion that it might be one of Drake's favorite hangouts. *Things are not always what they seem* kept echoing in her ears. Was the old woman referring to Drake or simply babbling nonsense?

Blue didn't believe in superstitions or any of the related mumbo-jumbo. The possibility that Drake had put the old woman up to saying those things was by far the most logical explanation. Still, it had unsettled her. And what had she meant by *there's something bad coming?* Was she referring to the general, who wanted his revenge on Drake? If she lent any credence to the woman's words at all, it was the part about being in over her head. Blue had definitely stepped in a little deep by allowing this crazy attraction to her principal to get a foothold in the first place. Neither she nor Drake appeared to have any control over it.

Blue'd had only one serious relationship in her life and that had just kind of fizzled out. Men didn't deal well with aggressive women, especially those working for the country's president. Her job had intimidated most of her male friends, other than those with whom she worked, and they treated her like one of the guys. She'd wanted it that way. The last thing Blue wanted under any circumstances was to be treated as anything other than what she was, a highly trained Specialist in the art of protection and a number of other skills that were classified.

But sometimes, to her self-disgust, the woman in her yearned to be treated like a woman...a real woman. The sweet, fragile kind. Then again, no man in his right mind was going to treat a female who could most likely kick his butt like a hothouse flower. Certainly no man wanted a woman like her for his wife or the mother of his children.

Regret pricked Blue, but she immediately banished it. This was the life she'd chosen and she had no real regrets...at least she hadn't until now. If a man couldn't love her for who and what she was, then too bad. She was too busy for a love life anyway.

Who needed flowers and candy or midnight phone calls or long, quiet walks on the beach?

Not Blue Callahan. She had a nine-millimeter, a .38 and enough attitude to keep life pretty damned interesting.

Who needed a man?

"Hello, Maggie."

The sound of Noah Drake's deep, rich voice shimmered over her, making her pulse react and her brain contradict her confidence in herself.

Blue touched her chest, feeling the small light stick beneath her blouse, drawing comfort from it. "You enjoy sneaking up on people, do you?" She strained, trying to see him in the darkness.

...the darkness will get you.

She forced away the old woman's words. The dark wasn't going to get her. She could run too damned fast to get caught by it or anything else. Besides, she had her light and her Glock.

Drake laughed softly. "I didn't think anything rattled you, Maggie Callahan."

She silently railed at herself for allowing the edge in her voice. He was the last person she wanted to know what scared her. "You annoy me, *Noah Drake,* you don't scare me."

"Is that right?"

He was right behind her.

She spun around expecting to find nothing.

He was almost invisible, his black clothes faded into the night like a chameleon's cloak. But that handsome face was plenty visible in a narrow spotlight provided by the moon, the lean, chiseled features a study in shadows and light. That carnal mouth almost smiling.

He stared down at her, those dark eyes drawing in the sparse light, glittering with it. Another velvety laugh. "I don't believe you, Maggie Callahan."

She ignored her brain's warning to back up a step. She would not give him the satisfaction. "Why do you do that? Call me Maggie Callahan?"

He watched her mouth as she spoke, only lifting his gaze to hers when she finished speaking. She barely restrained a shiver. He was doing this on purpose...goading her.

The smile stretched fully across that sculpted mouth. "Because it annoys you. I like it when you're angry." He laughed, more a breath of sound, but the amusement was clear. "It keeps you off guard."

She nodded once. "I see. I'm glad you're enjoying yourself at my expense."

He moved...closing the already minimal distance between them. It took every ounce of determination she possessed not to step back. "I didn't invite you here. You came into my world and refused to leave. All is fair in love and war, Maggie Callahan. And this is definitely war."

She lifted her face, looked directly into his eyes, ignoring the realization that only inches separated their mouths. "But you forget, Mr. Drake, we're on the same side here."

"Are we?"

The whisper of his breath across her lips was almost her undoing. She trembled in spite of her best efforts not to. "Of course. I'm here to protect you."

He looked at her mouth for so long that she almost

groaned with the effort of keeping her responses in check.

"And who is going to protect *you?*"

"Am I in danger right now?" she answered his question with a question of her own. Don't give him any more ammunition, she warned, the impulse to run almost overwhelming.

Another long, blatantly hungry stare at her mouth. "Very definitely."

A little hitch disrupted her breathing…an answering catch in his crumbled any bravado she had left.

Enough.

"Why don't you just go ahead and kiss me?" She looked straight into that startled gaze. "I know you want to. Just do it. Then you'll have it out of your system and we can get past this silly little game you like to play."

His fingers were in her hair, his palms cupping her face, so fast she felt dizzy from it. But it was his eyes that took her breath away. So much need…so much pain.

That sinful mouth lowered slowly toward hers and her heart lurched in anticipation. Her whole body tingled with it. Who was she kidding? She wanted this as badly as he did. From the first moment she'd laid eyes on him she'd wanted him.

Why pretend?

It was just the two of them in the darkness. Tension as thick around their bodies as the swirling fog.

His firm, full lips brushed hers and she gasped. God, if he didn't kiss her now…she would die. She would just die.

A twig snapped behind her. Twenty yards away maybe.

Drake's head went up.

Blue swiveled toward the sound.

Voices.

Male.

She flattened a hand against Drake's chest when he would have moved past her. She looked up at him and shook her head, simultaneously drawing her weapon. She gestured for him to stay, he only glared at her.

Ignoring his disapproval, she eased toward the voices. Slowly, carefully, not making a sound.

She glanced back once to make sure Drake wasn't following her. He'd disappeared again. Fear stung her at the thought that he might try to work his way around from the other side. She had to get there first.

Moving more quickly, Blue made her way toward the voices. Two, she estimated. Both male.

But one thing she'd learned long ago and had consciously chosen to ignore, unfortunately for her, proved true, haste makes one careless.

The rustle of leaves beneath her right foot, then the crack of a twig. She'd just given away her position.

Before she could move in a different direction, the muzzle of a weapon bored into her skull.

"Well, well, Blondie, fancy meeting you out here in the dark."

One of the two guys Chester had told Lowell about had referred to her as the blonde. It didn't take a rocket scientist to figure out who this bozo was.

"You're trespassing," she said succinctly. "And if that weapon you're carrying is a hunting rifle, you're in even more trouble than you know."

"Oh, yeah?" He jabbed her a little harder with the tip of the barrel. "Drop that gun you're carrying or you'll find out the hard way just what it is."

Not foolish enough to call his bluff, Blue set the safety on her Glock and tossed it onto the leaf-covered ground. She had her backup piece. "Satisfied?"

"Turn around," he ordered. "And put your hands up."

Her hands held high, she turned around slowly to face the man and his weapon. Before she got completely around, he grabbed her by the blouse and jerked her hard against him.

"You think you're one tough lady, don'tcha?" he demanded, his face in hers.

She looked straight into his eyes and said, "Yeah, I do."

He glared at her for a second, then looked to his left and shouted, "Over here, Jaymo!"

This guy she could handle, two might be a problem. She had to act now.

He grinned down at her, it wasn't pleasant, not even in the dark. "I think," he said eagerly, "we're gonna have ourselves some fun."

"You know what I think?" she said suggestively.

He jerked her closer. "What's that?"

"Not." She knocked the barrel of his weapon upward with her left arm at the same time plowing her right knee into his unsuspecting groin.

He hit the ground, dragging her with him.

The weapon discharged into the night.

Chapter Six

Blue's ears were still ringing from the rifle blast as she struggled against the man's weight. If he got on top of her...

Too late.

Her heart hammered faster, driving adrenaline through her bloodstream. She shoved at his chest with all her might, grunting with the effort, using the adrenaline to her advantage. She had to get him off. She kicked and flailed her legs, for all the good it did with him straddling her hips.

"Get off me, you son of a—"

"Well, now, Blondie," the sleazy bastard growled, leaning close, the smell of liquor thick on his breath, "he said you'd be a fighter."

Blue froze for one fraction of a second. The blood roared in her ears, blocking out all else. She pushed away the first thought his crude statement evoked. Lowell had said that Drake... She refused to believe that he would go to these lengths to be rid of her.

"Just makes things more interesting," the pig on top of her said lasciviously.

"You don't want to do this, pal," she warned, then tried to get in a punch, but he manacled her wrists and pinned her arms above her head before she could pull free. He crushed her hands together. The breath hissed between her teeth as pain seared all the way to her bones.

"Jaymo!" he called over his right shoulder. "Get over here, buddy, or you're gonna miss all the fun!"

Swearing under her breath, Blue twisted beneath him. Bucked. Anything to try and throw him off. He only pressed down harder, keeping her trapped almost effortlessly.

If only she could reach her ankle holster...

Relax, she told herself, forcing her body to still. If she relaxed so would he, then...

"Now." He stared down at her, his features scarcely visible in the night. His face was long and narrow, a thin, blade-like nose jutted out from its center. His hair was short and dark. The smell of sweat permeated his clothing.

"Let's see what we've got here." Holding both her hands pinned in a punishing grip against the ground with his left, he ripped open her blouse with his right. She stiffened, fear rocketing through her.

"Well, well. What's this?" He jerked hard on the chain around her neck, the metal biting into her flesh before snapping. He held the light stick up for closer inspection and rotated it slowly.

"Surely a firecracker like you isn't afraid of the dark?" He leaned toward her, using the dim glow from the light stick to inspect her face more thoroughly. He grinned, enjoying her discomfort or maybe looking forward to what he had planned for her.

She turned away. "Go to hell," she muttered. He'd better enjoy the moment because she wasn't going to make any of this easy.

"Come on, baby," he urged, grinding himself against her. Nausea roiled in her stomach. "We can do this the easy way or—"

She got her right hand free, plowed the heel of it hard into his nose. Screaming, he grabbed his face with both hands. Shoving with all her might, she propelled him backward. He tried to fight her off with one hand, using the other to hold his bleeding nose.

"Jaymo, you dumb bastard," her captor cried out. "Get over here!"

One swift kick to the head and her former captor, grunted then toppled to the ground.

Gasping for breath, Blue stared at his crumpled form for one long moment.

"Sykes! Where the hell are you, man?"

The other guy…Jaymo…maybe ten yards away.

She scrambled away from the slumped form and into the concealing undergrowth. She struggled to hold her breath…to keep from making a sound. Her panic rushed toward hysteria at the idea that it was dark and she didn't have her light. Her heart pounded so violently she was certain sudden death was imminent or, at the very least, someone would hear it.

Calm, she told herself. *Stay calm.*

The moon was still full. It wasn't completely dark. Tiny spears of light penetrated the thick overhead canopy here and there.

Not completely dark, she repeated silently as she retrieved her .38 from the ankle holster.

She was okay.

The friend, Jaymo, was stumbling around like a bull in a china shop. He was closer now. Hidden by the trees or the fog or both.

A new surge of the fight-or-flight chemical flooded her veins.

Drake.

Pete's sake, she'd forgotten all about him. Where the hell was Drake?

"It's safe now." His voice. Drake's.

Relief washed over her so quickly she felt weak with it. But what about the other guy?

Dammit. Drake could be an open target.

Blue lunged from her hiding place and almost stumbled over the jerk on the ground.

"There's another guy out there," she warned softly, peering through the darkness in the general direction from which she'd heard Jaymo's thrashings.

A leaf crushed beneath a footstep.

She whipped to the right.

Nothing.

Just the darkness.

"Where are you?" Her whispered words held a distinct edge of impatience. She was just about tired of Drake's hide-and-seek maneuvers.

"You don't need to be afraid," that silky voice assured her. "I've taken care of him."

Fury abruptly replaced all other emotions. "You were supposed to stay put," she said crossly. What was wrong with this guy? Did he have a death wish? she wondered as she crouched down to feel around for her Glock.

"If I'd stayed put," he commented dryly, his voice closer now, "where would that have left you? Two against one? Not very good odds."

She located her Glock, tucked the backup .38 into her ankle holster and pushed to her feet. "I can take care—'' he stood right in front of her...only inches away; she staggered back a step ''—of myself.''

Standing in a thin shaft of moonlight, the amused look on Drake's face was clear to see, telling her he was not convinced. ''Looking for this?'' He dangled the broken chain and light stick in front of her.

She snatched it from his hand. ''Actually,'' she snapped, ''I was looking for my Glock.'' To punctuate her words she shoved the weapon into its holster at her shoulder.

''I suppose we should tie up these two,'' he suggested, ''and call the sheriff.''

''I suppose.'' She checked the jerk, Sykes, who'd manhandled her for a concealed weapon. Nothing. The rifle was accessorized with a strap so she slung it over her shoulder. Rolling him over as necessary, she stripped off the guy's shirt and belt to use for restraints.

When Drake had dragged Jaymo to where she waited, she did the same to him, tucking his handgun into the waistband of her jeans. Using their shirts and belts, she secured the two men's hands and feet. They wouldn't be going anywhere.

''Are you all right?'' Drake asked when she was finally ready to head back to the house.

''I'm fine.'' It was a lie, but he didn't need to know that. ''Lead the way,'' she relinquished with a sweep of her hand. He would know the most efficient route to take and the sooner they returned to the house and made that call, the sooner these guys would get theirs. She was pretty sure they had nothing to do with Drake's situation. Just a couple of lowlifes with too much time on their hands.

To her surprise, Drake stayed close as they moved

through the dense woods and curling fingers of fog toward the house. She'd half expected him to disappear as he usually did. The realization that he was probably making it easy on her because she'd gotten roughed up only made her angry. She didn't need his protection. She was here to protect him. The jerk who'd pinned her to the ground had only momentarily gained the upper hand. She had taken him. She'd only needed the right opportunity.

Now Drake would no doubt think he was the protector because he'd gotten the other guy before she did. She'd just have to make sure he understood the chain of command here. He was supposed to follow her orders when it came to security. He hadn't, thus risking his safety in a situation she was perfectly capable of handling.

Lucas Camp and Edgar Rothman would not be pleased. She had to make sure Drake played by the rules from this point forward. She didn't need his heroics…though she had to admit that a tiny part of her was flattered. She forced that thought away. The last thing she needed was a foolish notion like that. She had a job to do.

And what the hell had gotten into her with that kiss proposition? Her face flushed with heat. She thanked God Drake wasn't looking at her right now. She'd asked—no, she'd told him to kiss her. What had gotten into her?

Yes, they'd both wanted it and the tension had been annoying. But there was simply no telling what he thought. Most likely he had come to the conclusion that she was a few cards shy of a full deck. And she couldn't blame him. She was more of a professional than that. The demand had simply popped out of her mouth before she could stop it.

His reaction had very nearly undone her. He'd taken hold of her so fast that it had startled her. Then he'd touched his lips to hers, just the slightest brush of skin, but she'd almost lost her mind at the contact. There was no way to pretend the desire away, it was there…strong and insistent.

As they emerged into the yard she couldn't resist a long look at the fog-embellished ocean. The sound of the waves lapping against the sand soothed her. Therapeutic, she decided. Just listening to it made a person want to forget the problems of the world. The moon hung so low in the sky it threatened to dip right into the water. She shivered, then hugged her arms around herself. How could danger lurk in such a beautiful place?

She looked up at the house and suppressed the urge to shiver again. The same ornate features that were appealing by day turned eerily haunting by night. She stared a moment at the shutter-clad windows that flanked Drake's bedroom—the tower room. Her imagination conjured his image on the widow's walk, looking out over the sea, yearning…wishing for what he could not have. She wondered how often he stood there and viewed the world to which he'd been sentenced?

No matter how beautiful, considering the vivid blue of the ocean, the pure white of the sand and the intriguing, albeit dark, emerald forest, this place was still a prison.

Life without the possibility of parole.

Life…alone.

The enormity of it was suffocating…overpowering.

He had no options, no goals or hopes. Only this place and the darkness. The painting she loved came to mind again. This was the kind of place, the kind of forlornness that the artist must have felt when painting it.

Noah Drake was like that.

She blinked, startled by the depth of her own emotions.

She turned back toward the house just in time to bump into the muscular frame belonging to the subject of her intense reverie. He stood near the steps, waiting for her to catch up, watching her every move.

"Sorry," she murmured, another blush heating her cheeks. Could she do nothing right in this man's presence? She closed her eyes for a second and sighed wearily, then forced her attention to the steps. She just needed to get inside and put this episode behind her.

Long fingers curled around her forearm, restraining her when she would have moved past him. "You're injured." When she looked up at him he touched her cheek, then the corner of her mouth. Worry furrowed his brow. "I should see to that right away."

An electrical charge skittered over her skin. She moistened her lips, for the first time tasting blood. She hadn't even noticed, but now the aches and pains made themselves known. Her back ached where she'd hit the ground. Her left elbow burned where it was skinned and her lip was busted.

"It's nothing," she protested as she pushed past him and onto the screened porch. She didn't have to look back or even hear him to know that he followed. She could feel him right behind her. He watched her with an intensity that unnerved her so completely that she felt at a loss to explain her reaction.

"What's happened?" Lowell demanded the moment they entered the kitchen. It didn't help that she deposited the confiscated rifle and handgun on the table. "Dear God, what is all that?"

Only then did Blue recall her torn blouse. She tugged the edges together, knowing full well she must look a mess. "You should call the sheriff. The two guys who did the careless shooting yesterday are tied up out there. A Sykes and a Jaymo." She glanced at Drake, who was still staring directly at her. "He can tell you where they are."

"Are you all right?" Lowell persisted as he followed her across the room.

She held up a hand to stop him. "I'm fine. Really. Call the authorities and everything will be fine."

Lowell looked at Noah, a question in his eyes.

Noah shook his head in answer to what he knew Lowell wanted to ask. "We left them bound and down for the count about a hundred meters east of the yard's perimeter. By the time a deputy gets here from the mainland they'll have regained consciousness. He won't have any trouble locating them then since they'll likely be screaming their heads off."

Lowell nodded, though he still looked hesitant.

"I'll take care of her," Noah said reluctantly, knowing that's what the older man wanted to hear.

"Perhaps she should call her superior," Lowell suggested before Noah could exit the kitchen.

Noah turned back and pinned him with a gaze that left no question as to the certainty of his words. "This has nothing to do with the general or why she is here."

Lowell conceded the point. "I'll make that call and take care of any questions."

Satisfied, Noah turned his attention to Blue Callahan. She didn't want to see him again tonight, he was certain. But she was not going to get her wish. This was his fault. Though the riffraff they'd encountered tonight had nothing to do with Noah or his past, still, she was here because of him and that past. Had she not been here, she wouldn't have gotten hurt tonight. Admittedly, he had wanted her to leave, still did, but he didn't want her hurt in any way.

Perhaps her injuries were only superficial, but they troubled him greatly. More than they should. That couldn't be helped. He'd thought himself incapable of such tender emotions. To feel them now, after all this time, for a woman he barely knew, surprised him. He fully recognized the error in the course he was about to take, but somehow he couldn't turn away from it. He had to go to her.

He hesitated outside her door, tried once more to discourage himself, but a force beyond his control would not allow him to walk away. He tapped on the door, hoping against hope that she would order him away…refuse to open the door…

"I'm in here."

Her muffled voice echoed through the closed wood panel obliterating any possibility of doing otherwise.

He opened the door.

Walked into the room.

Found her in the bathroom, dabbing at her injured lip with a damp cloth.

"I'm okay, really," she insisted, those deep blue eyes warning him not to come any closer.

He didn't stop until he stood right next to her before the mirror and sink. Her blouse lay open, torn and with the buttons missing. There would be a bruise on her left cheek by morning. Her silky blond hair was tousled as if someone had run their fingers through it over and over. His fingers fisted with the need to do just that. He'd plunged his fingers into her hair earlier. The feel of it haunted him still. Soft, silky.

He'd forgotten how smooth and velvety a woman's skin felt beneath his fingers. His loins grew heavy as he recalled those brief seconds when he'd cupped her face in his hands, grazed the warmth of her lips.

"You don't have to watch over me," she complained shattering the trance he'd fallen into. "I'm not a child or a damsel in distress, however hard that is to believe."

He felt the corner of his mouth lift in amusement. "I never considered you a child." His gaze roamed the length of her feminine body. Definitely not a child.

She tossed the cloth into the sink and planted her hands on her hips and glared up at him. "I'm no damsel in distress either, Drake. Get this straight here and now, I could have taken both those guys on my own. I've had all the right training. I know my business and don't you forget it."

He held up both hands in surrender. "Got it," he acquiesced. He'd been right, her eyes turned a good deal darker when she was angry. When she was calm they were blue like the ocean, serene and cool. But when her emotions flared, they turned almost cobalt blue.

She inspected the damage once more, leaning close to the mirror. Grimacing at her reflection, she dampened the cloth again with cold water and held it against her cheek. She muttered an expletive that precisely described the guy who'd done this to her. Her inventiveness made Noah smile.

"Would you like a brandy?" he offered, certain that she suffered from other pains not visible to him and that she would adamantly refuse to mention for fear of showing weakness.

She looked at him from the corner of her eyes, clearly suspicious of his attentiveness. "That would be nice."

Another warning went off somewhere in the back of his mind, but he ignored it. "Come with me."

He led the way to his suite, taking the stairs slowly. Opening the door, he entered his sanctuary, the third floor dungeon into which, until tonight, no other human had been allowed since Noah's retreat here. Not even Lowell was permitted on the third floor. Noah took care of things here himself. He preferred complete privacy.

He considered the woman following close behind him. She'd already been here, he reasoned. Uninvited yes, but she'd been here nonetheless. What would it hurt to have her here for the brandy? She needed...deserved a drink after what she'd been through.

It had been, after all, his fault.

Noah hated the way he rationalized his actions. He knew better than to do this...to think any of this. But the bottom line was he simply couldn't help himself.

Despite his circumstances, or maybe because of them, this woman was attracted to him. A part of him that had nothing to do with reason or rational thinking wanted to explore that...wanted to know why she succumbed to it knowing what she knew. He was familiar with her record, she was a professional all the way. These circumstances were as out of character for her as they were for him. That part intrigued him...made him desperate to know the why of it. Or maybe he just wanted to feel again.

It had been a very long time.

The realization that his body could react so strongly so quickly startled him as nothing else had since exiling himself to St. Gabriel.

"Would you like to sit?" he offered as he moved to the bar and poured her two fingers of brandy.

"No, thank you." She paused a few feet away, looking sorely uncomfortable and far too sexy, rumpled as she was from tonight's battle.

She was afraid of where this might lead. She was holding back…being the professional. He had to respect that. He handed the glass to her, reveling in the brief feel of her skin as their fingers touched. If she only knew what her mere presence was doing to him…

She sipped the liquor, closing her eyes and savoring the burn. Noah considered pouring himself a drink, but decided against it. He wanted to watch her…didn't want to miss a single nuance. Those eyes opened in a heart-stopping laser show of cobalt blue and he had to remind himself to breathe.

When she'd finished her drink and set the glass aside, she leveled her gaze on his. "We have a problem," she announced firmly.

Oh, yes. They definitely had a problem. But it was more his problem, he felt relatively sure, than hers. Every muscle in his body had hardened merely watching her drink. "And that is?" he invited her to continue.

"I asked you to stay put out there, you didn't. You could have been injured—"

He started to argue, but she stopped him with an uplifted hand. He deferred to her wishes.

"It's my job to keep you safe. As I told you before, I've been well trained. I know how to handle myself.

I don't need or want you getting in the way. I have a problem with failure. If you keep disobeying my orders I'm going to end up with a black mark on my record. I'd like to prevent that if possible. Do you think you can give me a break here? My boss is watching."

The fire in her eyes underscored her words. He understood perfectly. He'd been there before. Her career was top priority. Failure was not an option. She wanted to do her best, to excel, and he was getting in the way. There had been a time when he had felt just as strongly.

Noah considered her needs as well as his own for a few moments longer. She waited, clearly impatient, her hands still planted on her hips. Need so strong welled inside him all over again just watching her that he wasn't sure he could do with the proper finesse what he was about to propose. But there was only one way to find out if he could.

"All right, *Maggie Callahan,* I'll be more cooperative starting immediately, on one condition." Anticipation thrilled through him as he waited for her response.

That lovely blue gaze narrowed. "And that condition would be?"

An unfamiliar sensation coiled in his chest, a wide smile stretched across his lips. "That you agree to follow through with the offer you made earlier...before we were interrupted."

He recognized the instant realization dawned on her. Her eyes widened, her lips parted and the breath trapped in her throat.

"Mr. Drake," she began, shaking her head adamantly, "I—"

He shook his head slowly from side to side, cutting off the lengthy rebuttal to his suggestion she would have made. "No contingencies, no exceptions. All or nothing."

She chewed her bottom lip, unconsciously making him salivate. He wasn't sure he could hold out for her agreement. The notion of simply grabbing her and kissing her flitted through his mind, but he didn't want it that way. He wanted to do this kiss right...slowly, thoroughly.

He wanted her to know she'd been kissed.

Finally, she drew in a deep, bolstering breath and looked straight into his eyes. "One question."

He nodded once for her to continue.

"Is this a one-time thing or will you be requiring repeat performances?" she asked, her voice a bit stilted.

He inclined his head and pretended to consider the question, then he shrugged. "That possibility will remain entirely open. If one of us wants to do it again and the feeling is mutual, then we'll follow our instincts." He lifted one shoulder in a careless shrug that was in no way indicative of his feelings. "Bearing in mind that neither of us may want to do it again, we'll proceed under the impression that it's a one-time deal."

Something like indignation etched itself across the landscape of that pretty face. "Fine," she said tightly. "You have a deal."

"Fine," he echoed.

Three beats passed without reaction.

Then, just as he'd done before and in spite of his better intentions, he plowed his fingers into her hair, cupped her face and pulled her mouth up to his.

She tasted sweet and hot. Her lips were soft and pliable beneath his. Her fingers fisted in his shirt seemed to draw him closer, or maybe he just wanted to believe she did so. But then her lips parted...he thrust inside. His whole body jerked with need. It had been so damn long. The smell of her...the taste of her...he wanted more.

Kissing her would never be enough.

Her arms wound around his neck and she went on tiptoe, tilting her head back, drawing him more deeply inside that delicious mouth. He groaned, desire coursing through his veins and banishing all thought. He slid one hand down her back, molded his palm around her shapely bottom, pulled her more firmly against him.

Her palms flattened against his chest. He squeezed her bottom, feeling the savage roar of possession. She pushed against his chest. His mind denied the move. But then she pushed harder, forcing him away. She pulled out of his hold. His whole body reacted to the loss. He reached for her again, but she evaded his touch.

"I think that about covers it," she said as if completely unaffected by the kiss. "And remember, we had a deal. We both have to want it for that to happen again."

He blinked, tried to think...to pull himself back together.

"Thanks for the drink."

She walked out of his room without looking back once.

He scrubbed a hand over his mouth to try and stop the tingling there, it was no use. What the hell had just happened? He'd kissed her...lost all control...and she'd walked away as if the intimacy they had shared had been nothing at all.

A slow smile slid into place. He had a feeling that her little anticlimactic exit was all about control, putting him in his place so she could do her "job." Play the part of professional all the way. Well, two could play the control game.

Next time they kissed, she would be the one begging.

And he would show no mercy.

Chapter Seven

Blue jerked awake. Her arms and legs ached from sitting curled up so long in the overstuffed wing chair. She blinked rapidly to focus in the dim light of her room. She was alone. She shivered, recalling the dream that had left her feeling anything but alone. In the dream someone had been in the room with her...watching her...then touching her. She knew without question that her dream visitor had been Noah Drake. She had to stop thinking about him that way...even in her dreams. Lusting after the principal on an assignment was strictly forbidden.

She peered at her watch and realized she'd slept for a whole hour. She swore softly as she pushed to her feet and hurried from the room. That meant Drake could be anywhere, doing anything. She'd only meant to sit down and take her shoes off, but between the exhaustion left by the fading adrenaline and the warmth generated by the brandy, she'd dozed off.

What she needed was a long hot shower. Something to wash away the aches left by her scuffle with the fool carrying the hunting rifle and to distract her from the vivid memories of Noah Drake's kiss. She shivered again and called herself two kinds of fool. Not once in her career had she let this happen. Why now? With him?

Downstairs, she paused in the entry hall and peeked into the kitchen. Lowell and Drake were there... arguing.

"I don't like it." Lowell's voice. "This is just another reason she should call her superiors or, perhaps, Mr. Rothman. We can't be certain the timing is mere coincidence. What if they are connected to the notes? What if—?"

"I said no." Drake's voice held a distinct edge now. "End of subject. You said the sheriff's deputy knew those two guys and that they'd been in trouble for this kind of thing before. It's not connected to the general or to me. I've been more than patient with your harping, Lowell. I've even gone so far as to allow Miss Callahan to stay, but I won't be pushed any farther. Do we understand each other?"

"Of course," Lowell acquiesced.

An awkward silence followed.

Recognizing her cue, Blue stepped away from the door and moved quietly back up the stairs. Getting caught eavesdropping was about the last thing she wanted. For once she and Drake saw eye-to-eye. There was no reason to call Lucas. He would be on the island somewhere and was likely aware of the whole incident already. But he would not step in unless she needed him, and she didn't.

As a civilian, Lowell, of course, had no way of knowing that or understanding the way things worked. His only concern was for Drake's welfare and maybe hers. And probably his own. But the two men she and Drake had encountered in the woods had nothing to do with the general, of that she was certain. She'd read the general's dossier. He wouldn't play games like that. He would go for the jugular and be done with it. The whole notes thing just didn't fit his profile. But there was, according to the file, no one else who had reason to harm Drake. She supposed some local could be responsible, but she had to proceed under the assumption that it was the general. She thought of the latest note and wondered if he or some of his cohorts were actually here already. It would appear so since he was aware of her presence. But then, why bother with the notes?

...he said you'd be a fighter.

The jerk with the hunting rifle, Sykes, had said those words to her. Why hadn't she remembered that before now? Heat rushed through her veins and that was reminder enough. She'd been too distracted by the man she was supposed to protect. Had the guy's friend Jaymo assumed her to be a fighter based on his observations when they fired those shots at her yesterday? Or had someone else made the statement? That was a question she needed to have answered. Lowell had commented that Drake had said those exact words, but he had been as caught off guard by those two as she had. He couldn't be responsible.

Blue closed the bedroom door behind her and undressed as she crossed the room. The blouse was trashed. She tossed it aside and peeled off her tank top. Good thing she carried another chain because the one she'd been wearing was history as well. She toed off her shoes and rolled the socks away from her feet. The urge to walk barefoot in the sand nudged her again. She'd always loved beaches. That Noah Drake had his own private one was special in her book.

She shimmied out of her jeans and panties and

kicked them aside. A bra was something she never bothered with except when she ran or worked out. She found the garment far too confining. And since she usually wore a tank top or T-shirt under her blouse it wasn't a problem.

Completely nude now, she headed into the bathroom. That hot shower sounded better all the time. She was sore and achy. The hot water would relax her muscles and wash away some of the discomfort. She turned on the faucet and brushed her teeth while the water heated. Staring at her reflection she thought of the way Drake had kissed her. His touch had been strong, sure, but with an underlying desperation. His taste had been hot and male, filled with urgency.

It wasn't until he'd pressed her hips to his that she'd snapped from the haze of lust. She'd felt the fullness, the incredible hardness of his arousal and reality had broadsided her. Getting involved with him would be a major mistake, personally as well as professionally.

Their lives being worlds apart was the least of their differences. She had a gut feeling that his pursuit of the kiss was about far more than a mere kiss. He wanted...needed to prove something to himself. If he'd stayed completely away from all human contact except for Lowell, as she suspected, he was more than likely suffering from a serious craving to have sex. To prove he was still desirable.

No question there, she mused as she stepped beneath the hot spray of water. He was extremely desirable. She closed her eyes and allowed the water to rain over her, but her tightly clenched lids did nothing to keep away the images her mind conjured of the man.

Tall, dark and handsome was a cliché, but it described him perfectly. There was an allure of danger about him that was for the largest part born of the darkness that was his world. Even the locals had gotten that impression, considered him a vampire or other dark creature of which they had no understanding. Other than Lowell, whose presence he disregarded as much as possible if she had her guess, he interacted with no one.

But he showed no visible signs of being lonely, only bitter and resentful of outside interference.

A smoke screen, she decided.

His indifference and disregard for the human race was for show. Her eyes opened and she leaned her face away from the water, considering the concept more fully. He didn't miss what he refused to acknowledge.

So was the kiss an attempt to scare her off or a crack in his thus-far seemingly impervious control?

Blue reached for the soap and made a decision. She would know one way or the other whatever the cost to her. If he hoped to frighten her away, he could forget it. She'd had a lifetime of male domination tactics thrown at her, that was something she knew how to handle. But the other, well that might prove a little more dicey. Though she would very much like to see Noah Drake lose control and actually reach out to another human being, she wasn't sure she wanted to be the one he touched. Not if that touch was equally as intense as what she'd experienced tonight.

She wasn't sure any woman could survive him on that level with her heart intact.

Forcing the subject away, she lathered her body with the fresh bar of soap. She closed her eyes again and inhaled deeply. It smelled like spring, clean and fragrant. She slid the bar over her chest, down her abdomen, then reached between her shoulders.

The hot water pelted down on her skin, rinsing the sudsy lather away. Fire stung across her torso.

She hissed a curse and blinked to clear the water from her lashes. She stared down at her chest and abdomen. One thin red line after the other appeared on her skin, only to be erased by the blast of the water. It wasn't until she stepped back from the spray of water and the red drizzled and seeped from the numerous lines that she realized what it was.

Blood.

NOAH SPREAD the copies he'd kept of the harassing and threatening notes he had received during the past two months over his desk in the parlor. He studied each in turn. If the general was behind them, someone in Atlanta was mailing the notes for him. He wouldn't bother with such a trivial thing himself. In fact, in Noah's estimation, he wouldn't bother with the notes at all.

General Regan Bonner was a highly trained military strategist. Sending out warnings was definitely not his way. He would strike when he was ready, when his enemy was at his most vulnerable. He would not play games or drag out the inevitable.

Then who was behind the notes?

Noah stared at the cut-and-pasted words on the pages again. To his knowledge he had no other enemies. None who would bother with vengeance anyway. The locals were suspicious of him, that was true enough, but none of them had any real beef with him. None of them was aware of his past. Not even Lowell knew everything. He knew what Noah had told him, nothing more.

Only Edgar Rothman and perhaps his friend Thomas Casey or Lucas Camp knew everything.

Noah considered briefly that the whole scam could be a ploy to get at Edgar. Now there was a man who'd made more than his share of enemies. He'd gone head-to-head with numerous bureaucrats and agency heads over the years. But who would be privy to a failed experiment of this caliber? Who would have access to files so highly classified that even the president wasn't aware of all they entailed?

Noah's group basically did not exist and were so secretive that there was no organizational name. They were simply referred to as "the Others." General Bonner had discovered one of Rothman's experimental prototypes and had hoped to steal it for his own use. He had succeeded, the breach requiring desperate measures to rectify. The prototype, a chameleon-cloaking device, carried far too much potential for wartime use. As an espionage weapon it was priceless, its technology unparalleled.

Rothman had to get it back. But first he had to prove the general had taken it. Bonner, after all, had a prestigious reputation among his peers. Rothman's accusation was merely scoffed at.

There had been no other alternative. Someone had to get in, get the goods on the general and get the prototype back. A feat that, with the general's background in security and wartime strategies, would have been impossible unless the invader was, for all intents and purposes, invisible.

A second device was quickly made operational and then, for the first time, used on a human. A genetically enhanced, organic implant had been placed in just the right spot to override the brain's histological control over flesh and hair coloring. With a neurological base, the human guinea pig was able to invoke the process at will. The idea was that one could blend in with his environment. Of course, there were a couple of drawbacks. First, the subject had to be naked for it to work in any setting other than darkness. And, admittedly, the device did not work as well in most other environments. Second, since use in humans had not been tested prior to that, the side effects had been unknown.

Until five years ago.

Noah had been that guinea pig. He'd allowed the implant. He'd gotten the goods on Bonner and retrieved the prototype. And he was still paying the price.

There was only one side effect to the implant, which melded so fully with his own tissue that later removal was impossible—his body would no longer tolerate bright light. His flesh wouldn't spontaneously combust like the vampires in the old movies. He would simply suffer immeasurable pain. Every nerve ending would be charged with it to the point of overload. Prolonged exposure would result in a neurological blowout. Possibly a stroke, but ultimately leading to cardiac arrest.

Since there was no way to remove the implant without doing irreversible brain damage and there was no way to know how long it would remain operational, Noah had no choice but to live in darkness…in all likelihood for the rest of his life.

More than a year ago Rothman had approached him about a possible antidote of sorts—a neuron injection that would pinpoint the implant and shut down its function. The injection would work much like a heavy, intense chemotherapy treatment for a cancer patient. The only drawback was that Rothman couldn't completely rule out the possibility of shutting down other, vital areas of the brain. In other words, Noah could become a vegetable or simply paralyzed or any number of other things.

He'd refused the injection. At least he had control over all his faculties as well as his bodily functions. There was simply no compelling reason to take the risk involved with Rothman's antidote.

Noah had already made one costly mistake, he had no intention of making another.

Which brought him to yet another problem. Maggie Callahan. *Blue.* He closed his eyes and let go a heavy sigh. He should never have indulged his sexual fantasies. Drawing her into his life on a personal level was wrong, a serious error in judgment. He didn't even like it that she was involved on a professional level. But something about her made him lose all self-control. Made him want things he shouldn't.

He told himself that he could have this relationship with her and be safe. She would leave soon or the general would catch him off guard or both. Either way she would be free to carry on with her life and he would, if only for a short time, have felt something again. In addition, if he kept her close at hand he could see that she was protected.

Her job was top priority for her, but he knew General Bonner too well. He would never allow a single bodyguard, male or female, to stand in his way when he came after Noah. Blue's only chance of survival was if he kept her distracted and out of the line of fire.

What Rothman didn't understand about Noah was that he was prepared to face the general. He wanted

that over, one way or another. He didn't fear the man
or his minions. Noah had one very important element
on his side—this was *his* territory. He knew the island
like the back of his hand. The general would not beat
him here. Here, Noah's only enemy was the light, but
he had taken steps to ensure his safety during the daylight hours. He had an escape tunnel. The general
would never find him while the sun was up. Never.
Then the battle would be fought on Noah's terms. In
the dark…on his island.

"Your enemy has struck again."

Noah looked up at the sound of Blue's voice. She
plopped a plastic sandwich bag containing what
looked like a bar of soap onto the desk in front of him.
She'd showered and changed. Her attire consisted of
her typical fashion statement of jeans and a button-
down blouse over a sleeveless T-shirt. His gaze automatically skimmed the slender curves of her frame,
then her face. Tension vibrated from her. Her jaw was
tight…her lips in a firm line. Something was wrong.

More curious than concerned, he picked up the bag
and studied the barely used white bar. "It looks like
bath soap," he said distractedly still trying to determine why she'd bothered to bag it like evidence and
present it to him as if it held some mystery she was
yet to solve.

"It is. It was in my shower. I used it." The last
trembled from her lips.

His gaze shot upward to hers, the rhythm of his
heart picked up its pace. "What's wrong with it?"

She blinked rapidly to cover what looked like fear
or maybe pain. She held out her right hand, palm up.
"The soap contained a little more than cleansing and
moisturizing agents."

Her palm was scored with tiny lines that looked like paper cuts. His gaze moved from her hand to the bagged soap then back to her. A blast of outrage pushed him to his feet, sending his chair banging against the credenza.

He was around the desk and towering over her in one second flat. "There's more?" His voice was ragged with fury. He knew the answer without asking. How much of her body had she innocently rubbed the soap over before she realized...?

She nodded, her eyes wide with trepidation.

His jaw clenched so tightly a muscle flexed in protest there, he reached for the buttons of her blouse. She held perfectly still as he released one, then another and another until it parted, falling to her sides. But her choppy breathing gave away her internal response. His own body reacted in kind. His anger overriding all else, he focused on the task at hand. Above the scooped neck of her sleeveless T-shirt were more of the marring lines. He touched her skin, traced one thin line until it disappeared beneath the cotton of her top. She shivered, her flesh pebbling in goose bumps.

His throat went completely dry when he tugged down the neckline to find more of the scratches on the soft mounds of her breasts and in the delicate valley between them. His gaze lowered to where the hem of her T-shirt was tucked into her jeans. She gasped when he tugged it free. Lifting the soft fabric out of the way he surveyed her taut abdomen. More lines. She flinched when he touched the one that intersected her bellybutton.

Anger boiled up inside him so hot and so quickly that he could scarcely contain it. He snatched up the bag from his desk and removed the bar of soap.

"Careful," she warned, her voice still sounding breathless and shaky. "Slivers of what I think is glass are imbedded just beneath the surface."

Before the words were completely out of her mouth a cutting edge pricked him. He swore, then sucked the blood from his thumb. "I don't see how this could be." The other words he wanted to utter were too savagely vulgar to say in her presence. He carefully placed the bar back into the bag.

"We have antiseptic cream." His gaze moved back to hers. Dammit to hell, he hated that she'd been hurt yet again. Why not him? And how the hell had someone gotten into this house to do such a thing? It simply wasn't possible.

"I'm okay," she insisted as she straightened her blouse.

He shook his head. "We can't risk an infection." He strode to the door and shouted Lowell's name, then realized the time. Two in the morning. The man would be in bed. He rarely stayed up after Noah rose. Time had taught him that his company was not appreciated.

"We should check the rest of the supplies. If someone tampered with the soap, there could be more." He made a mental list of the items they needed to check. What he really needed was Lowell. He ordered all the supplies, knew the exact dates each order was filled and delivered. It would be difficult to get to the bottom of this without him. He wouldn't appreciate the intrusion, but Noah saw no way around waking him.

"It can wait."

Blue stood right next to him in the doorway, obviously reading his intent. "We need to know how this happened," he argued.

She sighed tiredly. "It can wait until morning. I'll

personally go through all the deliveries made to the house in the past few weeks. Lowell will help me.''

When the sun rose, Noah retreated to his rooms. It was safer there. The door was equipped with special locks. He didn't want to wait until morning. He wanted answers now. But she was right. Lowell's participation would be required. There was no point in disrupting his sleep. The damage was done.

''All right, that part can wait, but I insist on the antiseptic cream. That won't wait.''

She hesitated, but then nodded. ''Where is it?''

''Under the kitchen sink, where else?'' he teased. Didn't everyone keep the first-aid kit there?

''Where else,'' she agreed, finally smiling herself.

Noah followed her into the kitchen and collected the first-aid kit from beneath the sink. He opened it on the table and prowled through the contents until he found what he was looking for.

She reached for the tube. ''Thanks.''

He held it out of her reach and moved his head from side to side. ''I'm afraid I'll need to personally inspect and attend to the damage.''

She folded her arms over her chest. ''Look, Drake, I'm in no mood for games,'' she cautioned, her tone firmer now. ''So don't give me any grief here.''

''Take off your blouse,'' he ordered, ignoring her edict.

Her chin lifted indignantly. ''Are you nuts?'' She glared at him as if he'd just sprouted a second head. ''I'm not taking off my blouse for you.''

His body reacted instantly to the glimmer of desire he saw flash in those baby-blues. Good, he didn't want to be the only one affected here. ''Yes, you are. You grew up in a home filled with males, you're not shy,

I'm certain. Now stop wasting both our time and take it off.''

A flush crept up her throat and spread across her cheeks. ''I can't.''

When he'd touched her skin, checking for more marks, he hadn't missed the thrust of her nipples jutting beneath the thin cotton T-shirt. She wasn't wearing a bra...that was the problem. But, he doubted even that would stand in her way if he presented the challenge just the right way.

''This is all in the line of duty, *Blue*,'' he suggested trying not to sound overconfident. ''If you *were* just one of the guys, as you prefer to think, you'd have already peeled off that blouse as well as the T-shirt.''

Her gaze narrowed. ''I know what you're doing, *Noah*,'' she sassed, calling him by his given name for the first time. ''Don't think I'm so naive I can't figure you out in a heartbeat.''

The smile he'd hoped to keep concealed made an appearance. ''I'm sure I don't know what you mean. I have your welfare in mind, nothing more.''

''Yeah, right,'' she muttered. ''You just want to see my—''

''Is there some reason I shouldn't?'' He shrugged nonchalantly. ''Some malformation that you're ashamed of?''

Fury bloomed in her expression, but she did just as he'd known she would. She jerked off the blouse, allowing it to drift to the floor around her feet. She pulled the new chain holding a light stick over her head and dropped it next to the blouse. That, he decided, was her one weakness. Blue Callahan was afraid of the dark.

Before he could revel in his discovery, she did the

unexpected, she turned her back and peeled off the T-shirt.

Touché, he mused, exhaling on a chuckle.

"Just do it and get it over with," she snapped. She didn't have to turn around for him to know that she'd crossed her arms over her breasts.

Oh, she was tough all right. Tough as nails, but soft and sweet deep down inside. And that's where he wanted to be. He wanted to see if all that toughness would translate into wild hot sex. He was as certain that it would as he'd ever been of anything in his life.

Slowly, thoroughly, one line at a time, he applied a thin coating of the cream. Just enough to speed healing and to prevent infection. He touched her tenderly, lingering as long as he dared each time. She tensed with each new touch, sucked in an abrupt breath as if each time was the first.

"You'll need to turn around now," he said trying his best to keep the huskiness from his voice, but he failed miserably. His heart thundered mercilessly in his chest...his whole body was hard and aching. But he wanted more of this sweet torture...to touch her again...over and over.

At first he was nearly certain she intended to refuse, then, finally, moving one unhurried increment at a time, she faced him, her arms still shielding her breasts. Her eyes were huge, liquid with the same desire ravaging his body and soul. He wanted more than he'd ever wanted anything in his life to kiss her...to carry her to his room and make love to her. The resulting mental images evaporated the air in his lungs.

With monumental effort he forced himself to apply the cream to each line that marred the beauty of her delicate skin. He carefully painted all those on her chest, then moved to her abdomen. Her breath caught sharply when his fingers grazed the line of her waistband.

"Nothing lower?" he asked, his gaze colliding with hers.

She shook her head, her nostrils flaring with every rapid, shallow breath she took.

There was nothing more he could do with—

Before he could finish the thought, she slowly moved her arms away, her fingers remaining, concealing only her nipples, allowing him access to the soft mounds and valleys of her breasts. His hand shook as he touched first one and then the other, tracing the tiny red lines there.

When he'd finished they looked at each other for a long tension-filled moment. He wanted to kiss her again. She wanted it too…but he couldn't bring himself to do it. He'd goaded her into this and now he felt guilty…because he was as bad as the scum who'd torn her blouse only hours ago. He'd taken advantage of the situation.

He bent down and picked up her blouse, then gently draped it over her chest. "Good night, Maggie Callahan."

He was a better man than this.

Somehow during the past five years he'd forgotten who he was. But he knew that this was not who he had once been.

Maybe the man he used to be was gone…but he had no intention of becoming what he'd glimpsed just now.

Not even to have this woman.

Chapter Eight

Blue considered the two packages of soap lying on the kitchen table. She and Lowell had gone through everything in the house that wasn't nailed down. Food supplies, linens, paper items, cleaning products... everything. The only suspicious item was the package of soap. A three-pack, the ends of the paper wrappings had been opened, the bars tampered with, replaced inside the packaging and the ends glued shut once more so that no one would notice.

The soap had been purchased on the mainland in last week's order. As usual, Chester had picked up and delivered the list of supplies personally. There was always the off chance that the tampering had been done by someone totally unrelated to Drake, but that was a stretch.

Chances were, the tampering had taken place sometime after Chester had arrived back on the island with the goods. Lowell had called Chester's home repeatedly without reaching him, so he'd opted to take a ride around the island to find him. Lowell kept a ten-speed bicycle in the garage. He rarely used it, but had insisted on finding Chester ASAP. Like her, Blue saw, Lowell wanted to get to the bottom of this mystery as quickly as possible. His continued insistence that she should call her superior, Lucas Camp, grated on her nerves, but she tried to be patient. Something about Lowell didn't sit right with her. She frowned. It would come to her eventually.

Moving to the entry hall to await Lucas's arrival, Blue considered why she had waited until after Lowell had left to put in a call to him. It was always preferable to keep the profile of one's backup, or guardian angel, as low as possible. The fewer people who knew Lucas was on the island the better. That effort included Lowell and Drake, though she was certain both would be perturbed by her omission. Besides, she didn't want Lowell around making a bigger deal of this than it already was.

She'd tried hard all day not to think about Drake...but she'd failed miserably. The rush of forbidden emotions that surged through her each time she recalled his touch...his kiss, made her feel weak in the knees. She hugged her arms around herself and paced the long entry hall. Unless Lucas had discovered something new, she had gained no ground whatsoever in this case. She had succeeded, by the skin of her teeth, in persuading Drake into allowing her to stay. But that was about the extent of her accomplishments. There was nothing to learn from the notes he'd received. Rothman's personal forensics team had analyzed each and every one of them, to no avail.

Neither General Bonner nor any of his men, to their knowledge, had made a move to infiltrate St. Gabriel. There was nothing. And, yet, she'd been shot at, wrestled with, and ambushed with a bar of soap. Talk about a bad day...

And all that didn't even take into consideration that

she'd fallen into lust with the man she was supposed to protect—who'd spent more time protecting her than vice versa! Her reputation was going to hell in a handbasket here.

A tap at the door yanked her from her troubling thoughts. She checked the viewfinder and smiled when she saw Lucas on the other side. He was always a welcome sight.

She unlocked the door and drew it open wide. "Mr. Camp," she said by way of greeting.

"Callahan." He nodded and then stepped over the threshold, his cane supporting his weight on the right side.

Blue had heard rumors that he'd lost his right leg, from about midthigh down, while a prisoner of war. She'd also heard that there was a secret love in his life that somehow related to that past. A great deal of speculation was made by all the Specialists as to the kind of woman who could own the heart of a man like Lucas Camp. To say that he was somewhat extraordinary would be a vast understatement. Lucas Camp knew more about the spy business than anyone on earth. He probably knew more ways to kill the enemy than anyone else as well.

Yet, his compassion ran as deeply as his passion. If he showed half the passion in his personal life that he allowed in his professional one, whoever the lady was...she was one lucky woman.

Blue locked the door and showed Lucas to the kitchen. While he was here she would also turn over the latest note for forensics evaluation, for all the good it would do. Whoever was sending the notes, he was too smart to leave prints. But then again, even the smart guys screwed up at times. Drake would want it returned, like the others, but Lucas knew that

As she gestured to the soap on the kitchen table, she noticed that Lucas's attention was focused fully on her. "Who gave you the shiner?"

The bruise on her cheek pretty much extended up to her left eye. And then there was the healing tear in her lower lip. Funny she'd forgotten all about her busted lip when kissing Drake. Oh, and she couldn't forget the couple of dozen shallow slices in her skin, though most of those weren't visible. "One of the guys the sheriff picked up this morning."

Lucas nodded. He'd already been brought up to speed on that. "I take it the soap is responsible for the slice-and-dice routine," he suggested.

She self-consciously tugged at the lapels of her blouse, trying to hide the marks at her throat and above the scooped neck of her T-shirt. "Unfortunately."

It would have been impossible to miss the flicker of fury in those wise gray eyes. "Let's see what you've got."

Gingerly, she picked up first one and then the other bar of soap, showed him the imbedded slivers of glass and bagged each for taking to the lab. The one she'd used was already bagged and ready to go with the others. She then explained her theory about the wrappers with their reglued ends.

Lucas picked up one of the wrappers and studied it more closely. With no way to know just how many hands had likely touched it, obscuring prints was not a major concern. After he'd analyzed the exterior, he carefully opened it until it was a flat square of coated paper.

Blue hissed a curse as her senses rushed to another level of alert.

Cut-and-pasted letters, just like the ones on Drake's numerous threatening notes, spelled out the word *GOTCHA!* The second wrapper revealed the same, as did the one she'd retrieved from the wastepaper basket in her en suite bathroom. At least now they knew the threat was real. Whoever was sending the notes was serious.

"Okay." Lucas folded each wrapper and placed them inside another plastic bag. He focused his attention on Blue then. "Whoever is doing this is close. He, or she, is aware of your moves. Probably the two men you ran into last night were hired to spook you, though, as you say the sheriff suggested, they could have been simply local lowlife."

"But the soap, Mr. Camp. It seems illogical…a taunt versus real harm. I've checked everything else in the house. Every can, every package, every little thing. Only the soap was tampered with. Why not just make a real move on Drake?"

"The intended target was Drake, I'm certain," Lucas concluded. "It would tie into his condition."

A frown pinched its way across her forehead. She didn't like not knowing about his *condition.* "Why is that?"

Lucas averted his gaze briefly. "That's a question you'll have to ask Drake. I can't give you that information without breaching protocol." He searched her eyes for a time, trying to read more than she wanted him to. "Unless your reason is personal, there are really no grounds for you to know. That detail has no bearing on your ability to perform your duty. You know all you need to."

Blue was the one who looked away then. "You're right, of course. I'm just curious."

Lucas wasn't buying that for a second. He didn't have to say so, she read it in his posture and his expression.

A heavy sigh disrupted the silence that followed. "There's something wrong here, Callahan, and I can't put my finger on it. I don't like it. Not only is it not the general's style, it's too disorganized for anyone who'd plotted revenge for five long years. Tampering with soap that might or might not end up in Drake's shower. Sending the notes for weeks on end. It's as if rather than warning us, our player is baiting us, trying to reel us in to some sort of trap." His gaze narrowed as he mulled over his conclusions. "I can't shake the feeling that we're missing something right under our noses."

Blue had to agree. It did look that way…felt that way too. "Chester checks out," she reminded him, knowing where his thoughts had likely gone.

"So did Mr. Companion, Lowell, but that doesn't mean that one of them isn't hiding something. It only means that we haven't discovered it yet."

She shook her head in denial. "Not Lowell, Chester maybe. He thinks Drake is some sort of weirdo, even called him a vampire. Though he seems harmless, if I had to bet on one of them, it would be him. Lowell's been here for a year. He could have hurt Drake long ago." Or the old woman who'd issued her that warning, she didn't add. That little incident was still a little too creepy for her to bring up. She'd planned to broach the subject with Lowell, but things kept getting in her way…like kissing Drake or showering with broken glass.

"From now on you and Drake are only to eat what you have personally prepared. Don't swallow anything you haven't checked at least twice. Keep your head low, Callahan," Lucas warned as he gathered the soap and notes. "Don't trust anyone." He eyed her speculatively. "Not even Drake. He may have crossed a line, mentally speaking, that we're unaware of. That may be what we're missing."

As far as Blue could tell, the only person around here who'd crossed a line for a certainty was her, but she had no intention of saying so to the boss. Instead, she nodded. "Will do, sir."

She walked Lucas out. The dark sedan that had brought him waited in the drive. She arched an eyebrow in surprise. "Wow. How'd you rate such a cool ride?" Compared to Chester's truck, the sedan was a limo.

Lucas winked at her. "I have my sources, Callahan. When you've been in this business as long as I have, you know how to pull the proverbial rabbit out of a hat." He turned to leave, but glanced back before doing so. "Remember, I'm just a 9-1-1 away," he reminded, referring to his panic pager and their special code for help.

"Yes, sir."

Blue watched him go. For a man who walked with a prosthesis and a cane, his progress was efficient and fairly smooth, like that of all cunning predators. Anyone who thought Lucas innocuous because he had a handicap and had seen the better half of a century, should be warned. Lucas Camp was one-hundred-percent lethal when necessary. And all charm and grace the rest of the time.

He gave her one last nod before settling into the

back seat of the car. He even had his own driver, but the tinted windows prevented her from seeing who was behind the wheel. Lucas was too cool. Here she was struggling with the whole Gilligan's Island atmosphere and Lucas had a car and driver. She imagined he'd earned the right though...or simply taken it.

The car hesitated before moving down the long drive. Two seconds later Lowell pedaled his bicycle around the vehicle and into the yard. The sedan pulled away, disappearing into the camouflaging depths of the overgrown drive.

"Who was that?" Lowell swung his leg over the bike, removed his wide-brimmed hat and stared after the car, a frown muddling his expression. He lifted a bag from the basket, which Blue assumed held new and personally inspected soap. She'd sure be inspecting the bar she used from now on.

"That was my boss."

Lowell swiveled toward her, his eyes rounded in astonishment. "What?"

Incredulous was not an apt description of his reaction. *Shocked* was the better word. Confusion added to the mix of worrisome thoughts already troubling her.

She nodded. "He picked up the soap and the latest letter Drake received."

"Lucas Camp is on the island?" Lowell moved toward her, his startled expression gaining momentum rather than calming. "Already...I mean...now?" he stuttered. "I didn't know you called him."

She hadn't wanted to divulge Lucas's presence, but since Lowell had practically run headlong into him there wasn't really any way around it. He knew everyone on the island. Explaining away that car would have been impossible. Since Lowell knew Lucas's name, she had to assume Rothman had passed on that information.

"Is something wrong?" she queried. There had to be a reasonable explanation for Lowell's odd behavior. What did he care if Lucas was here? He didn't even know the man.

Composure fell too quickly into place and he smiled, the surface convention strained to say the least. "It's nothing and everything, I suppose."

Lowell gave a dramatic wave of his arms as if his burden was too immense to handle. "The whole thing is spiraling into the bizarre. Chester insists that no one but him had access to last week's order. He didn't stop anywhere or talk to anyone after picking up the items at the store. The boxes were never out of his sight." Lowell climbed the steps and stood next to her, peering out over the yard with a defeated sigh. "That leaves only you and me." He turned to her, his expression grave now. "I didn't do this terrible thing, Blue. I would never."

She dredged up a smile in spite of her uneasiness about his behavior. He was just as confused as she was. Upset too. "Somehow someone had to have gotten access before the goods arrived at the house." She chewed her lower lip and contemplated her next question. The last thing she wanted to do was unsettle him further. "Is Chester a drinker?"

Lowell shrugged. "He's been known to on occasion. But he has always been extremely reliable." He shook his head. "I'm sorry, but I'm inclined to believe what he says. Chester wouldn't hurt a fly. If he'd been drinking and perhaps allowed such a lapse in judgment by letting our supplies out of his sight, I believe he would simply say so.''

He certainly knew Chester better than she did. Maybe he was right. But, as Lucas said, something wasn't right here. The answer could be right under their noses. She thought of the old woman again. It was now or never. She had to ask Lowell about her. She looked toward the forest on the north side of the house, the area where she and Drake had run into trouble last night. ''I ran into someone else in the woods last night,'' Blue began, hoping like hell this wasn't going to sound as crazy to him as it did to her.

''Oh?'' His questioning gaze connected with hers when she faced him once more. ''Besides the riff-raff?''

She nodded. ''An old woman. She warned me that something bad was coming and that I should be very careful. She even called me by name.''

Lowell looked skeptical. ''What did this woman look like?''

Blue thought about that for a moment. It had been awfully dark. ''Her skin was mahogany almost, maybe she was African-American, I can't say for sure. She wore a lot of jewelry and—'' she gestured to her head ''—something tied around her hair, like a bandanna maybe. The most distinguishing feature was a scar—'' she traced a line across her cheek ''—from the corner of her eye to the edge of her mouth. It looked pale against her skin, you couldn't miss it even in the dark.''

Lowell went ashen. ''The old voodoo woman?'' The words were barely audible.

Blue shrugged and made a sound of uncertainty. ''I don't know who she was. Just an old woman who, oddly enough, knew my name. I guess she kind of looked like someone who dabbled in voodoo.''

Lowell was shaking his head now. ''That's not possible. The woman you're describing is dead. She died about thirty years ago and is buried behind the old chapel. I've heard the tall tales about her. She's definitely dead.''

Drake's words about the old voodoo witch rang out in her head. She laughed, the sound tight, maybe even a little nervous. But she didn't believe in that stuff. ''Look, I know what I saw and this old woman was *definitely* alive.''

Lowell reached for the door to the house. ''Maybe the darkness or the moonlight played a trick on you. With the fog we had last night, sometimes your imagination runs away with you.'' He frowned when he noticed the door wasn't locked.

''I just came out to see Lucas off,'' she explained as she followed him inside. He didn't respond, just locked up as usual. No matter what Lowell thought was possible or impossible, she knew what she'd seen, fog or no fog. The old woman had been real…and very much alive.

NOAH STOOD on the widow's walk, camouflaged in the darkness. He'd risen more than an hour ago, but he'd chosen to stay in his rooms rather than join the others downstairs. He wasn't ready to face her again so soon. He wasn't sure he ever would be. So he'd worked.

He'd hardly slept at all this day. His own actions where Maggie Callahan was concerned troubled him greatly. He'd kept his distance for all these years…been strong and now that strength seemed to diminish with each breath he took, with every moment she stayed.

His thoughts were consumed by her. He wanted to be with her more than he wanted anything else. It was absurd. He barely knew her...certainly couldn't feel anything beyond physical attraction for her. Yet it felt like so much more. His traitorous emotions scarcely considered the reasons she had come, his complete attention perpetually fixated on her alone. The threat of death be damned.

How foolhardy was that?

Then, it wouldn't be the first time he'd been a fool. He'd spent what constituted the best part of his lifetime putting his career before all else, focusing solely on the job. What made him think he would show better judgment now, in exile? All that had saved him these past five years was total segregation.

He had no right to draw her into his private world. It was bad enough that she was here in a professional capacity. To play upon her feelings...her attraction to him...was wrong, selfish. He understood that and still he could think of nothing else. He wanted her with a desperation that minimized all else into insignificance.

This was a decision she had to make. In order to do that she had to know all the facts. If, after being made aware of his circumstances, she chose to pursue this path, so be it. Becoming involved with him would be a mistake, but it was hers—hers alone—to make if she so desired. And when her time here was up, she would go.

Decision made, Noah went in search of her.

He found her in the living room scanning the perimeter of the yard via the monitor that was a duplicate of the one in his room. It had been set to nighttime use, which eliminated the numerous filters that blocked the brightness of the sun during daylight hours.

Before making his presence known he studied her for a while. He liked very much that she always wore her hair down. Her clothes were far too concealing for his taste. He would like to see her in a great deal less fabric, fabric that was much more sheer. Actually, he'd like nothing more than to see her completely naked.

She turned abruptly, as if he'd telegraphed that last thought to her. The moment she became aware of his presence her tension grew palpable. The bruise on her cheek had darkened. Anger seethed inside him again. Not for the first time he wished it within his power to hurt the man responsible for that mark as well as the others. He thought of the way he'd touched her early this morning, applying the antiseptic ointment, and he longed to touch her more intimately.

First, he had to know that's what she wanted. Before she could make an informed decision she had to know the full truth. She had to know everything. Primarily that there was no future involved.

"I hope you slept well," she said, her tone guarded. She was uncertain of this ground, and he could understand that, considering his conflicting signals.

"Not very." He paused next to her. "And you?"

Those blue eyes locked fully onto his and need welled inside him. "I didn't sleep at all," she admitted. "Lowell and I spent the entire day making sure the food supplies and so forth were safe."

"I take it you found all to your satisfaction?" She was treading carefully here, keeping the conversation on business.

"Everything but three bars of soap that were delivered last week. Chester insists that the supplies were never out of his sight, yet the glass was imbedded in all three and all were made to look as if they'd never been opened.''

He filed that information for later analysis. ''Anything else?''

''Inside each soap wrapper there was a note. Cut-and-paste jobs like the others.''

He waited expectantly for her to continue.

''Gotcha!'' She searched his eyes, for reaction no doubt. ''That's all. Just that one word.''

Noah scrubbed a hand over his chin, belatedly noting that he should have shaved, but he'd had no patience for it. ''I think I'd like to speak with Chester myself on the matter. Lowell as well. Has he retired already?''

She nodded. ''I think he was pretty tuckered out from all the excitement.''

''We had a visitor,'' Noah prodded. He'd been aware of the intrusion, but had not wanted to interfere. He'd recognized the man from Edgar's description of him. The infamous Lucas Camp. The man inspired awe in most, hatred in a few. But everyone in the business had heard of him. He was a legend.

''Lucas Camp, my boss.'' She massaged her forehead with her fingers, tired and sleep-deprived. The exhaustion was only now catching up to her, the struggle was visible. ''He believes we're missing something right under our noses. He wants to dig a little deeper into Chester's background as well as Lowell's.''

Noah lifted one shoulder in a shrug. ''Though I doubt he'll find what he's looking for in either of those gentlemen, I agree that we are overlooking something."

He tried not to devour her with his eyes, but the task was a difficult one. He wanted to study every line and curve of her. To know her by heart. No matter what else happened.

"No one on the island has ever given you trouble in the past?"

That angle had already been pursued, but he wasn't opposed to repeating the exercise. "There are a couple of the locals who at first resented my presence since they didn't understand my circumstances. They made a few idle threats, threw rocks at my house, nothing drastic. In time they simply gave up and accepted that I was here to stay."

She looked directly at him now, her eyes earnest. "And what *are* your circumstances, precisely?"

He motioned to the sofa. "Please, sit down."

She held his gaze, unmoving, trying to read him, assess his intent, but he gave away nothing just yet. Finally, she relented and perched on the edge of the sofa looking anything but relaxed.

He selected a seat directly across from her. He wanted to see the reaction in her eyes when he told her what she wanted to know. What he needed her to know.

"Five years ago a prototype cloaking device was stolen from Edgar Rothman's research group. The device, in the wrong hands, posed a serious threat to national security. I agreed to retrieve it."

"The general stole it," Blue offered.

"Correct." Some parts she already knew. Now for the hard part that she didn't know. "In order to retrieve the prototype, I was forced to use a duplicate device. The mission could not be accomplished without absolute anonymity." Flashes of memories from those moments when he'd insisted on the mission flickered past his mind's eye. Edgar had tried to dissuade him, but he'd known as well as Noah that it was the only way.

"But something went wrong," she suggested when his silence dragged on.

"Yes. The device is an organic implant that overrides the part of my histology and neurology that controls flesh tones, hair coloring..." He splayed his hands in a magnanimous gesture. "At will I can take on the qualities of my environment, to an extent. I can blend in. The dark is the most favorable environment."

She blinked, attempting to hide her initial astonishment. "Still?" She shook her head. "I mean, does it still work?"

He nodded affirmatively.

A flicker of irritation darkened those blue eyes. "That's why I can't see you when you go out into the darkness. You used it to hide from me." She huffed an exasperated breath, then seemed to catch herself and tuck her annoyance away. "But there are complications? Side effects?"

"Yes. The implant affected my nervous system in such a way that it remains oversensitive to light. If I'm exposed, there is severe pain that eventually leads to death."

Her expression turned solemn, fearful...fearful for him. "So you're not safe in the daytime. If someone tried to flush you out...you'd be at his mercy. They could storm the house, drag you out."

"I've taken measures against that." He gestured to

her. "You're here to see that no one is able to do that." He wasn't prepared to tell her about the escape tunnel just yet.

"I'm not enough." She pushed to her feet. "You're too vulnerable in this house. If someone came after you...there are ways to draw you out."

"There are ways, yes." He stood, moved toward her. "No one is exempt from the dangers of everyday life. I live in a prison as it is, I refuse to resort to even more desperate measures. I won't run from him."

She stared up into his eyes, the emotion in hers something unfamiliar to him. "There's no way to undo this implant thing? They can't just take it out?"

"No. It's organic. It melded with my own tissue far more quickly than anyone had imagined. Attempting to remove it would result in far worse consequences."

"There's nothing they can do?"

Noah should simply say no, but that would be a lie. He didn't want any untruths between them. "Edgar Rothman has developed an injection that he believes would shut down the implant, but it carries a great risk as well. There is a very strong possibility that it would damage other areas of my brain. I will not take the risk."

She looked away from him and shook her head. "So this is forever?" Her gaze shifted back to his, demanding an answer.

His heart stumbled at the regret he saw in her eyes. But he did not want her pity for what he could not change. "Yes. It's forever."

She laid her hand on his arm. "Thank you for telling me. It means a great deal that you shared this with me. I prefer to be fully informed in order to be more prepared for an assignment."

He looked down at her, his gaze leaving no room for speculation. "I didn't tell you this to better prepare you for your assignment, Maggie Callahan," he said bluntly. "I shared this information with you because I want you to understand that I'm offering you no strings...no future...nothing beyond here and now." He reached up to touch her. Her breath caught. His fingertips traced the softness of her cheek. "I'm only offering this moment, if you wish to take it."

For the first time in more than five years, Noah had put his emotions on the line. She would never know the courage it took him to do this...to ask her to accept him as he was, for what he was, for just this one moment.

She backed away from his touch, her eyes going liquid with emotions, sympathy, compassion, pain, all the things he did not want to see.

"I'm sorry, Mr. Drake," she said, her words scarcely a whisper, but all too telling. "I can't do that."

And then she walked out, taking something he'd felt certain no longer functioned beyond the involuntary and purely physical...

His heart.

Chapter Nine

It was almost dawn and still Drake had not come out of his room. Lowell had told her that it was Drake's custom to roam at night. It was his only freedom…his only means of escape. In the darkness he was untouchable.

Blue had thought that knowing all the facts would help her to fully understand and to focus better on the mission, but that was far from the case. Knowing the sacrifice he had made for his country and the pain he had suffered as a result only made her more aware of him as a man. She had certainly known her share of selfless males. Her father and brothers had all chosen the course of public service, putting themselves in the direct line of fire to safeguard their neighborhoods and cities. Any one of them would be willing to lay down his life for another. She felt the same way. Had proven her loyalty to the job on numerous occasions.

The reality that Noah Drake continued to suffer, watching the world from inside his prison as life passed right by him, tugged at her heartstrings no matter how hard she tried to be objective. She told herself repeatedly that he was simply her assignment and that she was here to do a job and walk away when it was over, but it didn't help. Somehow, from the moment she'd first laid eyes on him, something had shifted, some strange connection had fused. It was as if she'd known him for months instead of days. She couldn't explain it, she only knew that it was there.

In spite of his seeming nonchalance about his personal security, she wanted desperately to keep him safe…to make all this right for him. But he wanted more. If she was brutally honest with herself, she wanted more as well. That just couldn't happen. Her entire life she had prided herself in her work, focused completely on it. Sure she wanted the house in the suburbs and the pitter-patter of little feet…someday.

Just not today. She had dreams to fulfill. Goals to reach. She couldn't possibly give up everything and be happy in a remote place like St. Gabriel. Not that Drake had asked her to. In fact, he'd made it very clear that his proposition involved a physical relationship only. He hadn't had to say those precise words, she'd understood completely.

It had cost him dearly to go out on that emotional ledge and make the offer. She'd hurt him by declining…rejecting him. Blue closed her eyes and let go a heavy breath.

She didn't want to hurt him. But, either way, she would. Whatever decision she'd made would have ultimately meant heartache for both of them. When Lucas called with another assignment she wouldn't be able to say no. How could a man like Drake be happy with a wife who rushed off to play hero more days out of a month than not?

Of course, he hadn't asked her to marry him. He'd asked her to have sex with him.

She thought of the way his kisses had melted her

insides…of how his body had felt against hers. It was definitely a tempting offer. But it would be a huge mistake for both of them. She would never be able to have a physical relationship with a man like Drake without falling in love with him. She knew that if nothing else. Not to mention the distraction it would lead to. She couldn't afford to be distracted. Until the threat was pinpointed and neutralized Drake's life depended upon her…as did her own.

No matter how she rationalized it, no matter that she knew she was doing the right thing, she had to make him understand that her decision had nothing to do with a lack of desire or with any lack on his part. She had to set the record straight.

Blue chafed her arms and shivered as she moved through the long entry hall and toward the stairs. The clock chimed then struck three times announcing the hour. She was tired, she needed a few minutes sleep, but she wasn't sure she could risk the downtime until Lowell was up and about. Surely she could make it three or four more hours.

The bloodred runner muffled her steps as she climbed the sweeping staircase. She'd almost gotten used to the eerie gloom of the house. The dim lighting gave everything an other-worldly appearance 24/7. It reminded her of an old Hitchcock film. There could be most anything lying in wait around the next corner.

She slowed, frowning, as she passed Lowell's room. The door was closed but a bright glow filtered from beneath the door. She remembered his warning that even flashlights were forbidden. Apparently it was do as I say not do as I do because the light spilling from under his door was definitely brighter than the designated watts. She considered knocking, but then thought better of it. If he'd been reading, he might have simply fallen asleep with the extra light on. There'd been enough stress in the past couple of days, there was no point in making bad matters worse for no real reason since the light was confined to his private quarters.

She climbed the second staircase a bit more slowly, dread pooling in her stomach. Not that she had any misgivings about seeing Noah, to the contrary. She enjoyed seeing him a little too much. However, she did not look forward to the inevitable confrontation in regards to his earlier proposal.

Be that as it may, she had to do the right thing here. She wasn't a coward. She thought again about the old woman who'd warned her that something bad was coming. Blue had never been a superstitious person, but every time she heard the jangle of those spirit bottles or thought of the old woman, she got the willies and had the urge to cross herself. God, she was becoming her mother.

Overreacting was not her usual MO. Maybe the perpetual lack of light was wreaking havoc with her ability to keep her head on straight. Her hormones were definitely unbalanced.

She rapped on Drake's door and waited, straining to hear any sound. Nothing. She supposed he could be on the widow's walk. He seemed to really like that spot. Though she'd never been up there she was sure the view was spectacular.

No answer.

She knocked again, her instincts going on point.

Nothing.

If he'd sneaked out of the house without telling her...

She tried the knob; it turned.

Holding her breath, she opened the door and pushed it inward. The room looked even darker than before. She wondered vaguely if there was a dimmer switch somewhere. Or maybe it had just felt lighter with his presence. She reached for the light stick beneath her blouse and gave it a little shake. The answering glow took her stress barometer down a degree or two.

The room smelled like him, she noted as she moved through the dark space. Clean and masculine, but with an underlying mysteriousness that escaped her ability to describe—something leathery or earthy.

"Mr. Drake," she called out when she encountered no sign of him. She didn't want to be accused of snooping again.

No answer.

The instinct that he was not here nagged at her. His presence was somehow energized...magnetic, and she didn't feel that right now. There was a definite emptiness...a void that only he filled.

Blue sighed and silently railed at herself. She was falling for him already and they had only kissed. What was wrong with her? She just wasn't the type to swoon over a handsome man, not even a dark, mysterious one. Maybe her mother was right and her biological clock had kicked in, screwing up her hormones in more ways than she knew. She needed that like another hole in the head. She was on a mission, there was no time for feminine weaknesses.

Right now she was a Specialist...being a woman wasn't supposed to be relevant.

"Mr. Drake?" she called again.

Not a sound.

Dammit all to hell.

When he returned to the house, which he would have to do soon, she intended to give him a dressing down he wouldn't soon forget. She'd warned him about going off on his own without telling her. As he'd pointed out, however, he was pretty much safe in the dark. It wasn't like anyone could see him if he didn't want him or her to.

Blue froze in the center of the room.

For that matter, he could be watching her right this minute from just across the room. She turned slowly and squinted into the darkness. She could vaguely make out the shapes of furniture. The bed, a chair, an armoire. The sitting area she remembered from her previous visit. But all detail was obscured.

She was almost certain he wasn't in the room. Her instincts couldn't be that far off the mark. Well, she decided, if he could break her rules, she could break his. Maybe she would do a little snooping.

Moving soundlessly, she entered the bathroom, which was not quite so dark. As in her bathroom, there was a restored clawfoot tub, an ornate pedestal sink and then a more modern glass-encased shower. The other necessary fixtures were in keeping with the antiquity of the house. Smooth, cool tile covered the floor and part of the walls. It looked to be beige or off white. If there had ever been a window, there wasn't one now. His scent permeated the room. The fresh masculine soap and that other musky, earthy fragrance that was his alone.

The next door led into a large walk-in closet. Inside was a well-stocked wardrobe that was all black, shoes included. For blending in to the darkness, she presumed. At the end of the clothing racks was something unexpected, another door. She crossed to it and only hesitated a moment before opening it. She shouldn't...she knew she shouldn't. But she just couldn't help herself.

For a long time after entering the secret room she simply stood there and stared at what she saw. She'd noted the state-of-the-art ventilation system and the worktable. The faint smell was unmistakable, the supplies lying about irrefutable evidence, but it was the other, larger items that took her breath away—blew her mind.

Noah Drake was an artist.

Canvas after canvas, stacked three deep, sat on the floor along the walls. One was framed and hanging on the wall. The beauty of it drew her closer. It was a spectacular view of the ocean at night, most likely from the widow's walk. He'd captured the moonlight glinting on the softly rolling waves perfectly. The infinity of it, bordered on both sides by trees and mist, the stillness, the sense of waiting. It was beautiful, hauntingly so. And in all that beauty she saw the loneliness of the man who'd painted it. Though he never, for one second, allowed her to see or feel it in him, here it was, savage pain and longing captured with each stroke of the brush.

Everything inside her went very still as recognition slowly unfolded inside her.

She knew this work. The heart-wrenching, draw-you-in-and-swallow-you-up depth of it.

Her gaze dropped down to the bottom right-hand corner and her breath caught in her throat. N.D.D. Noah David Drake. His full name had been in his profile. She'd read right over it without a second thought.

She turned away from the beautiful painting and moved around to the front of the easel that stood in the center of the room. Propped on the stand was a work in progress...

Her image.

The air that had trapped in her throat rushed from her in one long whoosh. She forced herself to breathe. The vague scent of oil paint and mineral spirits filled her lungs. He was far from finished but the eyes left no doubt as to the subject.

Something inside her shifted, clicked as if finally connecting fully. This was why she'd been drawn so strongly to Noah Drake from the very beginning. She'd been in love with his work for months. She'd sat in that gallery and studied that one painting of the forest for hours on end. Any time she wanted to relax, to lose herself between missions, that's where she went. The painting drew her into another time and place where a man who could only be as haunting and alluring as his work must surely be.

And he was.

Here. On St. Gabriel. This was why something about the place had felt familiar to her. The connection just hadn't fully cemented. She knew this place, knew this man.

Taking another deep breath to calm her racing heart, Blue forced herself to leave the room. She closed the door behind her and stood in the closet for a few moments to allow her eyes to adjust to the slightly dimmer lighting.

This was what Noah Drake did with his time. She now also knew how he earned at least part of his income, the paintings. The gallery owner had told her that his showings were always a sellout, but no one knew who he was or even his real name. Only N.D.D. The works were all sold through an agent in Atlanta.

The owner had intended to keep the piece Blue had purchased, but she'd finally, after months of putting up with Blue's obsession with the painting, agreed to sell it to her.

Blue moved toward the bedroom door with the intent of hunting Noah Drake down and demanding to know why he hadn't shared this wondrous secret with her as well. Surely if he was prepared to have a sexual relationship with her he could have told her this. Then again, he had insisted on no strings.

Well, she would just tell him what she thought about that in a New York minute.

A hand clamped over her mouth. Instinctively she reached for her weapon. Another hand manacled her wrist. Adrenaline rushed through her veins.

She twisted, used her right leg to unbalance the body holding her firmly against it.

They went down…hit the floor. Two simultaneous grunts echoed in the silent room. She twisted…almost broke free. He rolled her over, scrambling to get on top of her. His hand moved away from her mouth. She screamed, prayed Lowell would hear her. Kicked with all her might. Struggled to free her arms, which were pinned beneath her.

The hand came back. Pressed a cloth over her mouth and nose. She tried to shake it off. Bucked to throw him off. She couldn't breathe…strange odor.

Her body went limp.

Fabric rustled as he moved off her.

She tried to move…then…nothing.

NOAH MANEUVERED through the darkness toward home. He was running behind schedule. If Blue had noticed him missing she would be furious.

He clenched his jaw. He refused to care if she was angry with him. He told himself that her rejection did not pain him, but it was a lie. He wanted her desperately, felt that same want in her, but she denied its existence.

Not that he could blame her. She was fiercely dedicated to her work. At one time he had been as well. To pretend otherwise would be just another lie. She was right and he was wrong. Allowing this thing between them to escalate beyond the professional was a mistake. He should be thankful that she'd had the good sense to say no.

But he wasn't.

In all fairness he would not hold the decision against her. It was hers to make. His own selfish interests had driven him to toss out the offer. How could he fault her for making the right decision?

He couldn't.

But he didn't have to be happy about it.

The house was too quiet when he entered through the screened porch. Usually Lowell was up by now and pacing the floors waiting for Noah's return. Especially when he was late as he was this morning. Noah had spent a good deal of the day and part of the night painting. But then he'd had to get away from the house. Had to feel the wind on his face and smell the salt air.

His work in progress had forced him away. It wasn't bad enough that he was infatuated with the woman…he had to go making her the subject of his work.

Bringing her to life on canvas was like touching her intimately. He grew hard just thinking about it, even now—after an exhausting run and hours of walking aimlessly.

Noah's frown deepened as he moved through the parlor and back into the entry hall without encountering anyone or hearing any sounds of habitation.

He froze, his gaze riveted to the front door.

It was ajar.

He moved to the door and swung it wide open. There was no one outside as far as he could see. No automobile. He closed the door and locked it, then listened intently. Not a single sound. Lowell knew the rules about keeping the door locked, as did Blue. Both were conscientious about seeing that it was done.

Fear rushed through him.

He bounded up the stairs and was halfway down the second-floor hall when he came upon Lowell. He was attempting to pull himself up from the floor, using the wall for leverage.

"What happened?" Noah demanded as he assisted him in getting to his feet.

Lowell cried out in pain when Noah moved his right arm. "I think my arm is broken," he groaned.

"Tell me what happened," Noah insisted, fighting for calm. "Where is Miss Callahan?"

Lowell braced himself against the wall. "I don't know. I heard her scream and I came out of my room and someone attacked me from behind. I didn't see anything."

The older man turned toward the staircase that led to Noah's quarters. "The scream came from your room."

Ice forming in his chest, Noah followed his gaze. "Go into your room, Lowell, and lock the door," he ordered without ever taking his eyes off the stairs.

"You can't go up there," Lowell said, clearly frightened. "There could still be someone there."

Noah's gaze collided with his. "Miss Callahan is up there."

Horror claimed Lowell's expression as if he'd only just realized what the scream he'd heard meant. "Oh, dear God."

"Lock your door," Noah repeated as he started toward the stairs. Fear of what he might find…or that he couldn't help her roared through him. He didn't have a weapon…only his ability to disappear into the darkness.

By the time he reached the third-floor landing he was prepared to enter the room as stealthily as a shadow.

The door stood open. The lights were turned so low that they were very nearly off. That would work to his advantage. His night vision was so well developed that it would not hinder him in any way.

Blue lay on the floor in the middle of the room. His heart pounding, he moved to her side. Her pulse was slow and steady. No visible signs of injury. Thank God.

He rose and moved about the room to ensure the threat had passed. The door to the widow's walk stood ajar. He opened it and checked the area. Nothing.

Certain that whoever had broken in was gone, he adjusted the light setting to the full wattage allowed and hurried back to where Blue still lay unconscious.

Three seconds of fierce concentration later and he knelt beside her, his body as visible as hers. He was glad that now had not been one of those times he found it difficult to make the transition back to normal. Gently, he rolled her onto her back and checked her body thoroughly for unseen injury, broken bones and the like.

As his hands moved over her she roused. "What...what're you doing?"

She pushed up and tried to scramble away from him, her eyes wide with fright and confusion.

He held up his hands in a calming manner. "It's all right. You're okay. Whoever attacked you is gone now."

A frown marred her forehead. She rubbed a hand over her face and shook her head. "I came in here to find you and he came out of nowhere, wrestled me to the floor and then drugged me with an inhalant."

Noah picked up an object from the floor. It had, apparently, been under her. "He left you a gift."

Her gaze focused on the voodoo doll in his hand. It was black with a lock of long blond hair wrapped around it. Blue's blond hair, Noah was certain.

"You're sure it was a man?" he asked, his gaze connecting with hers.

She nodded. "I'm positive."

The lights had been set so low when he'd come in the room he couldn't see how she could be so certain. "The room was almost completely dark."

She pushed to her feet. "I'm positive it was a man," she said more firmly, irritably in fact. He supposed if he'd just been drugged he would be a bit irritable as well.

Noah pushed to his feet, watching her closely. The next thought that occurred to him sent fury roaring through his veins. "Did he...?"

The look in her eyes told him he didn't have to finish the question. "No. But I felt him—" she cleared her throat "—against me. He was aroused."

Fury…outrage…there was no word to describe accurately the depth of the emotion ripping him apart inside. He crushed the doll in his fist, wanting to do the same to whoever had done this to her. He didn't care that somehow someone had trespassed in his home. He only cared that they had touched her.

"I want you to leave. Today." He spoke slowly, struggling to keep his words even, a semblance of calm in his tone. "I don't need your protection. I can take care of myself."

She threaded her fingers through her hair and exhaled a heavy breath. "We've been through this before, Drake," she refuted firmly. "I'm not leaving until the threat to you is neutralized or I'm reassigned." She cocked her head and glared defiantly at him, daring him to rebut her proclamation.

A new blast of outrage stiffened his spine. "Fine. Then you'll be reassigned. Rothman brought you here, he can send you away."

Noah gave her his back and left the room. He would call Edgar now. He wanted her out of here today.

Final decision made, Noah double-timed it back down to the second floor and paused at Lowell's room. He tapped on the door. "It's safe to come out, Lowell. We need to call Chester to come take you to the mainland to have your arm seen to."

The door opened slowly. Lowell peeked out before opening it all the way. "I can probably get there on my own," he offered, always sensitive to putting anyone out.

Noah shook his head and surveyed the older man for other injuries. "No, it might not be safe for you to go alone. We'll call Chester. Dawn is upon us, I'm sure Chester will be up."

Noah ignored a seething Blue who followed close behind him. The sound of her soft voice tugged at his senses as she questioned Lowell about his encounter in the hall. It appeared that both had been attacked by the same person. Both insisted the house's exterior doors had been locked.

Whatever the case, Noah was taking no more chances. Lowell and Blue were leaving. He would face this alone. He should have insisted on this to begin with. Edgar had pulled a fast one on Noah by sending Blue, and then he'd been so intrigued by her he had not sent her away immediately. A mistake on both their parts. Noah wouldn't put it past Edgar's having asked for a woman, perhaps even this particular woman, in hopes of stirring emotions in Noah.

Well, his plan had worked.

Too well.

But it was over now.

The loud pounding on the front door made Blue gasp as they descended the main staircase.

Resisting the urge to look back at her, Noah hesitated at the bottom of the stairs and waited for Blue and Lowell to catch up with him. He kept his eyes carefully averted from hers.

"The two of you can wait in the living room while I see who is here."

Blue placed a hand against his chest. "I'm the one with the gun handy."

Noah lifted a skeptical eyebrow. "That doesn't appear to have been a great deal of help to you thus far."

Her full lips thinned in anger. "Step aside, Drake, I'm getting the door. Besides, the sun is rising."

Realization jolted Noah with her words. He'd been

so overwrought with concern for her and for Lowell, that he'd completely forgotten this damned curse.

She inclined her head toward the stairs. "Go back to your room. Lock yourself in. We'll take care of this." She withdrew her nine-millimeter.

"Check the viewfinder first," Noah insisted, determined to know the extent of the threat, if any, before he left them alone with it.

She huffed a breath, then did as he asked. "It's Lucas!" She turned to Noah. "Did you call him?"

He shook his head. "No." And he hadn't. His call was going to be to Edgar. He wanted Blue and her people off this island *today*. "But since he's here, invite him in. We have things to discuss."

Noah retired to the parlor where any light let in by the opening of the door wouldn't reach him.

Blue glowered at his retreating back. She had never in her life met such a stubborn man. Then she thought of those heartrending works of art in his secret room. Her anger dissolved, leaving only the raw emotions she knew would serve no purpose. But she simply couldn't push them away.

She drew in a bolstering breath and opened the door. "Mr. Camp, is something wrong?" She tried to sound calm and businesslike. At the moment she was too worried about what Noah intended to say to her boss.

Confusion lined Lucas's brow. "I received your 9-1-1. What's going on here?"

"What?" She stepped out onto the porch and pulled the door closed behind her, not wanting Noah to overhear. "I didn't send out a call for help."

The purple and gold hues of dawn stretched across the lush green lawn and the black sedan parked there.

A thin mist still clung to the air, reminding her of the night before last's adventure in the woods with Sykes and Jaymo.

"I don't know what's going on, Callahan," Lucas began, "but I don't like this at all. Who had access to your pager in the last half hour?"

The memory of being rendered unconscious by an intruder exploded inside her head.

Someone was watching every move she made.

Someone who had the means to gain access to the house.

A prickling sensation on the back of her neck sent her instincts soaring toward alert.

"We should go inside," she suggested, scanning the yard once more. "I've got—"

A high-pitched *crack* rent the air.

Her mind analyzed the sound instantly.

Gunshot.

High-powered rifle.

A second shot.

Lucas stumbled forward, a startled expression on his face. His cane clattered to the wooden floorboards. Just as Blue reached to grab him and pull him into the house, he crumpled in her arms.

Chapter Ten

"Shut the door!" Blue shouted to Lowell.

"What's happening?" he cried, hysteria rising in his voice as he cowered on the far side of the hall, cradling his arm.

Ignoring the question, she eased Lucas down onto the floor and kicked the door shut herself.

Two wounds.

Left shoulder. Left thigh.

Thank God it wasn't the right one. He'd suffered enough loss there. But the left was his good leg and it was bleeding heavily.

She swore softly. "Call..." Dammit, they were on an island. Who did one call on a frigging island?

"Ramon..." Lucas stirred enough to lift his head to look toward the door. "He was in the car." Lucas groaned and dropped his head back to the floor. "Are you hit?" he asked Blue. He sounded breathless now, panting to keep the pain at bay.

She shook her head in answer to his question. "I'll check on Ramon, but first we've got to get you some help."

Lucas dismissed her concerns with a wave of one hand. "Check on Ramon *now*. I'll live but—"

"Lowell, call Mr. Venable," Drake said as he knelt next to Lucas, cutting him off mid-protest. "Tell him we need a ride to the mainland right away. Call Emery and Chester as well. Emery isn't much of a doctor but he'll do. And alert the authorities in Savannah, they'll need to have an ambulance waiting. If they can get a medflight over here, that's even better. But we don't want to wait if there isn't one available."

While Drake gave the necessary orders to Lowell, Blue rushed to the kitchen for a couple of clean hand towels and the first-aid kit—for all the good it would do. She thrust the items at Drake and said, "Try and stop the bleeding. I'm going out there to check on Ramon."

He snagged her arm and shook his head. "Don't go out there. Chester will be here soon."

The worry in his dark eyes touched her but she didn't have time for that. "I have to do this. You just take care of my boss."

Drake delayed her a moment longer, but finally nodded and released her from his powerful grip.

"Be careful, Callahan," Lucas called weakly, then swore as Drake started inspecting his wounds.

Blue saw that Lowell, careful of his injured arm, was making the first of the calls as she hurried through the kitchen and to the back door. She couldn't open the front door and let in the light with Drake in the entry hall.

Setting her Glock on ready, she eased out the back door. She was fairly certain that neither of Lucas's wounds was immediately life-threatening, but still she had to neutralize the threat so that he could be moved to a hospital as quickly as possible.

At the corner of the house she listened for several seconds.

Nothing.

Quickly but cautiously she moved around to the front of the house. Moving stealthily from one position of cover to the next, she made her way to the car. The driver's side-door was open. No Ramon.

The sound of gunfire echoed from deep within the woods. Her gaze whipped in that direction.

Ramon had given chase. She ran hard and fast, not bothering with stealth now. Dodging trees and thick clumps of undergrowth she was halfway to the old chapel when the scene unfolding up ahead brought her up short.

Ramon was flat on his back on the ground. The other man stood over him, a high-powered rifle in his hand pointing directly at the center of Ramon's chest.

Blue aimed her weapon. If she called out to the man he might fire anyway, killing Ramon. If she took the shot...

Decision made, she fired.

The man dropped like a fallen tree and Ramon scrambled from beneath him.

Blue rushed to his position. "You okay?"

Dusting himself off, Ramon got to his feet. He was a thin man, forty maybe and with a distinct Latin heritage. He was hilarious under normal circumstances. All the Specialists loved him. He was part of Mission Recovery's Housekeeping Team.

"I am now," Ramon said tartly. He checked the dead guy and retrieved the rifle. "What took you so long? I thought that backwoods bubba was going to kill me for sure."

Blue winked at him. "I can't believe you let a guy

like that get the upper hand on you.'' She glanced at the guy on the ground and shook her head. Jaymo. One of the guys from the other night.

"He wouldn't have if he hadn't sneaked up on me while I was taking care of his buddy.'' He gestured toward a crumpled form a few feet away.

She checked the second downed man. Sykes. "Been there, done that,'' she admitted. "I knew these two were hiding something. They've tried to take me down twice already.''

Ramon's expression turned somber. "Is Lucas…?''

"He's okay. But he needs a hospital.'' She glanced back at the two men they'd left on the ground. "Good thing those guys are such bad shots.''

Ramon's gaze locked with hers. "Or maybe it's just supposed to look like they are. These guys are either professionals or were instructed on exactly how far to go by someone who knew precisely what he wanted to accomplish.''

She frowned. "You're sure about that?'' She'd gotten the exact opposite impression.

He nodded. "Positive. They try to come off as ya-hoos, but the hit was too well organized. I think it was planned down to the letter. They weren't trying to kill Lucas.''

As they sprinted back to the house, Blue considered Ramon's conclusion. But if Drake was the ultimate target, none of this made any sense at all. And why would Lucas be the target? What was the motivation? If he was, why wasn't he dead?

The notes were addressed to Drake. The glass slivers in the soap left no question as to the identity of the target. Things just didn't add up. Unless the target on that occasion had been her. That was just too off the wall. Then again, maybe she wasn't thinking clearly. In her defense, she was running on empty as far as sleep was concerned and she felt a little groggy still from the inhalant that had been used to put her under.

Maybe Ramon was right.

Within minutes, she and Ramon had Lucas loaded into the back seat of the sedan. Lowell climbed into the front passenger side. His arm needed serious medical attention and he was behaving damned strangely. Giving him grace, he was injured and had just been in the middle of a shoot-out. But this level of hysteria just wasn't in keeping with his usual demeanor. He'd said that Emery and Chester were nowhere to be found, but Mr. Venable had agreed to be ready at the dock to take them to the mainland. Lowell had also called the sheriff and told them about the two men in the woods. The same ones they'd released less than twenty-four hours prior, he'd added.

After locking up, Blue stood in the entry hall and tried to ignore the exhaustion clawing at her. She had to report Lucas's injury. Casey would need to know ASAP. She needed substitute backup. She scrubbed at her forehead with the heel of her hand. And she could sure use some sleep, if only five minutes worth.

Noah saw the weariness creeping up on Blue. Without some rest she'd likely collapse soon. Though he was certain she'd fight it every step of the way.

"I'll take the first watch," he offered. "You catch some shut-eye. I'll wake you in a couple of hours or as soon as I hear from Lowell on Lucas's condition."

"I'm okay," she insisted. "I have a couple of calls to make."

He stayed her when she would have moved past

him. "We both need sleep. Taking turns is the only reasonable solution. Don't argue with me on this one."

Her gaze met his and he saw the uncertainty there. "There is one thing we need to get straight. I went to your room this morning to talk to you."

Noah wasn't sure he wanted to hear what she had to say. He was suddenly certain it was about his foolish proposal. That had been a mistake. He knew it now. This latest turn of events had proved clarifying.

"What do we have to talk about other than who'll take the first watch?"

She closed her eyes and sighed. The defeated sound tugged at him. "Don't make this harder than it already is. *This* is who I am. It's what I do."

She said the words firmly, but there was a plea in her eyes when she opened them once more.

He nodded in surrender. "All right. What is it you need to say?"

"Declining your offer wasn't about you. It was about me and who I am…who I need to be." She shrugged those slender shoulders. "For me, right now, my career comes first. A relationship with you would go against everything I hold as a standard for myself." She touched his face. He tensed, but only for a fraction of a second. "Trust me, Drake, if we'd met under other circumstances, I wouldn't hesitate. This just isn't the right time."

The feel of her skin against his made him tremble inside. "It was a mistake. A temporary lapse in judgment. It won't happen again," he said curtly. He couldn't allow himself to make the same mistake twice.

"Mistake or no," she said, drawing her hand away,

"we have business to finish when this is over. I'll make my calls then take the couch. I don't want to be far away. You wake me at the first sign of trouble. If anyone approaches the house or calls…anything." She sighed wearily. "I need to know that Lucas is all right."

"You have my word."

When she'd settled on the couch, Noah made a few calls of his own from the kitchen out of her hearing range. The first was to Edgar Rothman. He wanted Blue out of here immediately. Whatever had to be done to make that happen, he wanted it accomplished. Her safety was too important to him.

"Things are only getting more dangerous for you," Edgar argued vehemently on the other end of the line.

"I can take care of myself." Noah's voice was coldly insistent. Somehow Edgar just didn't get it. "I want you to cut them loose now…today."

Edgar's sigh was audible. "And if Bonner shows up and kills you, how am I supposed to live with that?"

Rothman blamed himself for Noah's dilemma. No matter how much Noah argued with him on that point. "This is my decision, Edgar, just as the one I made five years ago was mine alone. It isn't your fault."

Silence vibrated across the line for one awkward moment. "I wish you would consider the treatment, Noah. I really believe it will work, otherwise I wouldn't be so adamant about it. You could have your life back."

Noah's chest constricted at the thought. He wanted his life back. He wanted Blue Callahan. But, if he took that risk, he might lose everything. At least he had his work. That and his ocean kept him sane. He wouldn't want to live if his condition worsened.

"The answer's still no," he stated firmly.

Tension filled the next stretch of silence. "All right. I'll tell Casey that I want him to abort the assignment, but not for forty-eight more hours."

"Edgar—"

"No buts, Noah. I'll be there day after tomorrow. We'll talk face-to-face then."

He hung up before Noah could argue.

Edgar coming here in person wasn't going to change anything. But at least he was going to call off Casey. Lucas Camp had already been injured. Noah didn't want anything happening to Blue. All he had to do was keep her out of the line of fire for forty-eight more hours.

He checked to make sure that she was sleeping, then he ensured that all the doors and windows were locked. After that he climbed the stairs. Something had been nagging at him from the moment he found Lowell on the floor. Something that didn't quite fit.

Noah was naturally suspicious…it was the nature of the beast in the business he'd once been in. Few things ever slipped under his radar. That someone this close to him could have fooled him didn't seem plausible. Still, he was no fool. There had been far too many coincidences lately. Ignoring the possibility was out of the question.

BLUE JERKED AWAKE. She glanced at the wall clock and realized she'd slept just over an hour. She stretched as she got up, thankful for the reprieve, but ready to jump back into the fire. A frown worked its way into her expression when she considered that Lucas should be at the hospital by now. Why hadn't Lowell or Ramon called to give her an update?

Maybe one of them had, and Drake had opted not to wake her. In which case, she'd have no choice but to kick his rear. She almost smiled. No, that wouldn't work. Touching him in any way would only give her too much carnal pleasure. She thought about the way his beard-stubbled jaw had felt beneath her fingers and she shivered. Nope, a good tongue-lashing would have to do, and even that conjured ideas that were off limits.

At the top of the stairs she surveyed the second-story hallway and moved quickly toward Lowell's room. She could no longer ignore her mounting suspicions about the man. Something wasn't as it should be. The comment he'd made—calling her a real fighter, saying Drake had said it—and then hearing that same remark from the guy who'd taken her down in the woods. Lowell's odd reaction to hearing that Lucas had been at the house. His even more peculiar behavior after Lucas had been shot. Behaving uncharacteristically hysterical. Obnoxiously so. And then suddenly, the moment it was time to get in the car to take Lucas to meet Mr. Venable. Lowell was calm as could be. Of course, he had been injured and frightened. She supposed...

No, that wasn't right either. In her gut, she knew that Lowell was hiding something. No one else had access to the house. Too many unexplainable events had occurred. Chester had sworn that he hadn't taken his eyes off the supplies before delivering them to the house. Whoever had attacked her only hours ago had gained entry into the house without force. It just didn't add up. She and Lowell were the only ones with keys.

Either someone was using Lowell, somehow coercing him into going along with their plans, or he was one of the bad guys.

Blue froze in her tracks when she thought about Jaymo and his pal Sykes in the woods. Lowell had called the sheriff. Lowell had said that according to the sheriff the two were nothing but local yahoos who'd done this sort of thing before.

No one else had spoken with the sheriff's deputy.

No one else had even seen him.

Who was to say that the deputy had ever even been called or that the two men had ever been in custody and interrogated.

Only Lowell. She hurried now, rushing toward Lowell's room.

All she needed was one scrap of evidence—

She slammed into a hard male body in the open doorway. She jerked back, reaching for her Glock…

It was Drake.

She exhaled the breath that had stalled in her lungs. ''Sorry.'' She released the nine-millimeter's grip and displayed her palms stop-sign fashion. ''I'm a little edgy.''

He smiled, just a ghost of a gesture. ''Understand-able.'' Then he frowned. ''You should still be rest-ing.''

Focusing on his words rather than the movement of those incredible lips proved a real challenge. ''I couldn't sleep any longer…there's something I need to check out. No word from Lucas or Lowell yet?''

He shook his head. It dawned on her then that Drake was standing in Lowell's doorway and that wasn't nor-mal.

''Something's been nagging at me as well,'' he said,

then stepped back for her to enter the room. "I think you should see this."

The ominous note in his tone sent goose bumps pebbling over Blue's skin. She followed him into the room.

"Look closely at the photographs on the walls."

Blue had assumed they were of family, but closer inspection revealed the truth. "They came with the frames."

Noah nodded. He took down one of the frames and removed the back. Lowell had carefully matted the paper photo so that the size and price information imprinted there was covered.

Five photos had been treated in that manner. He'd carefully chosen different frames that used similar images for display. The people looked so similar, no one would have noticed unless they had been looking for discrepancy.

She remembered on the first day she'd arrived, assuming that this was likely his room. She'd noted the framed photographs, but hadn't looked at them closely, and, considering the low lighting, especially before her eyes had grown accustomed, she hadn't noticed anything unusual. She remembered that he'd mentioned losing his family. She just assumed these photos were of the family.

"Does this smell familiar?"

Noah held out a handkerchief. She lifted it to her nose and cautiously sniffed it. Drawing back instantly, she coughed and purged her lungs of the strong stench.

"It was him."

The words were hers, but she barely recognized them as her own. She shook her head in disbelief. Though she'd mentally noted several inconsistencies in things Lowell had said and done, it was still hard for her to believe that he could play his part so well. What on earth did he have to gain by doing this?

"Take a look at this." Noah opened a drawer in the bedside table and showed her the mutilated magazines, glue and other items needed to create threatening notes.

"Why would he do this?" she voiced her disbelief and frustration, then chewed her lower lip as she turned the idea over in her mind. "It doesn't make sense. He's lived here with you all this time. He could have killed you on numerous occasions. Why do the notes thing and all this other cloak-and-dagger hoopla? Could he be connected to the general somehow?"

"I don't think this has anything to do with me."

Realization burst through all the other confusing thoughts. *Lucas.* It was about Lucas.

"He's got Lucas," she murmured almost to herself. "I have to warn Casey and—"

Noah placed a restraining hand on her arm when she would have rushed from the room. "There's more."

Ice-cold fear thickening her blood, she watched as Drake picked up an innocuous-looking shoebox that lay on its side, the contents spilled across the chenille bedspread.

"Look at these." He picked up a handful of photographs, mostly candid snapshots, and a few five-by-sevens.

Blue's heart pounded harder with each photograph she viewed. One by one she shuffled through the stack. Dozens of shots of Lucas, but always in a crowd or an unapproachable situation. There were other subjects pictured as well. The only other one that stood out was that of a woman. There was photograph after photograph of her as well. Late forties, early fifties, attractive, dark hair with a hint of gray. Very sophisticated looking. Then there were a couple of the woman with Lucas.

Though Blue didn't know the woman's name, she knew instinctively that this was the woman who owned Lucas's heart. The woman all the Specialists speculated about.

"How long did you say Lowell has worked for you?" she asked, as she reviewed the photographs once more. A sinking feeling had started deep inside her.

"One year. Before that I managed without anyone else. But after—" He hesitated as if unsure whether he wanted to divulge the rest. He swallowed tightly. "After the accident I knew I couldn't really manage on my own so I sought out someone to take care of details…just to be around on a regular basis."

Worry twisted inside her. "Accident? What kind of accident?"

He stared at the floor a moment. "I had the flu or a bug. It dragged on and on. I ended up dehydrated, got dizzy one evening and fell in the kitchen." He rubbed the back of his neck. "Lay there unconscious for an hour or so before I came around. I'd hit my head in the fall. There was a lot of blood. Scared Chester worse than it did me. He brought Emery to patch me up. I pretty much admitted the need to have someone around at that point." He laughed dryly. "Well, actually, Edgar insisted."

Blue almost said good, then realized that Lowell was the assistant—companion or whatever—who took the job.

"I got used to having him around eventually. It was

his idea to contact an agent...when he stumbled upon my hobby.''

His artwork. He still didn't want her to know about it. That stung just a little, but she had no time to dwell on it. ''Who recommended Lowell?'' There had to be a connection.

''I ran an ad in the classifieds. Conducted the interviews myself. Lowell impressed me. His background check was clean so I hired him.''

Lowell had impressed her too, at least as far as his concern for Drake. She laid the photographs near the shoebox. ''I have to get word to Director Casey. We're going to need an entire team.''

''I agree. I'll—''

A loud pounding on the front door echoed all the way up the stairs.

''Stay here,'' Blue said for all the good it would do.

She ran down the hall and descended the stairs two at a time, Drake right behind her. He ducked into the parlor, away from the possibility of being exposed to the light.

When she checked the viewfinder Chester stood on the porch. Drawing her weapon, she unlocked and opened the door. ''What's up, Chester?'' She scanned the yard, found only his old truck.

He didn't look surprised at all by her weapon. Instead he hitched a thumb in the general direction of the road. ''I'm here to find out what the devil's going on,'' he grumped. ''Old man Venable said he'd been waiting over an hour at the dock and nobody showed. Then when I come to find out what the trouble was I saw a black car'd been run plumb off the road.''

Renewed fear surged. ''Was there anyone inside?''

Chester pushed back his cap and scratched his head. "Just one Mexican-looking feller. I can't say for sure, but he looks dead to me."

Ramon.

Blue jerked Chester inside and closed the door. "What kind of injury did he have?" she demanded, Chester's shirt lapels held tightly in her grip to keep his attention.

He tapped his head. "There was a lot of blood."

Damn. "I've got to go out there," she told Drake who had joined them in the hall the moment the door closed. She released Chester and bent down to retrieve the .38 from her ankle holster then handed it to Drake. She didn't want him unarmed for even the time it would take to unlock his gun cabinet. "Chester will go with me. Call and see if we can get some sort of medflight here just in case Ramon's alive. Whether he's alive or not, Chester will drive him to the dock. There should be enough room on the beach there for a copter to sit down." She looked hard into Drake's eyes. "Once you've made that call lock yourself in that secret room of yours."

To his credit, he didn't look at all startled that she knew about the room. "I'll be back," she assured him.

Before she could unlock the door, he pulled her to him and kissed her hard on the mouth. "Be careful. We have unfinished business."

She nodded stiffly, noting somewhere in the back of her mind that she'd said those words to him earlier.

Once Drake was safely out of the entry hall, Blue and Chester left. She locked the door behind her, double-checking that it indeed locked before she joined Chester in his truck.

Not a half mile from the driveway, the black sedan

sat half in and half out of the woods. Blue bolted from the truck before Chester came to a full stop. She jerked the driver's-side door open and checked Ramon's carotid pulse.

"Thank God," she breathed. It was there, weak and thready, but there.

"Can we move this car?" she asked Chester.

He went around to the front of the vehicle and checked it for damage. "Should be able to."

"Okay. Let's get him scooted over to the passenger side and you can drive him to the dock and wait for the medflight." She prayed like hell one was available nearby, like in Savannah. "I'll take your truck back to the house."

"Okey-doke." Chester opened the passenger-side door and with Blue's assistance scooted Ramon over.

She quickly stripped off the blouse she wore over her tank top and used it for a makeshift bandage around his head. "Once you get stopped at the dock, I want you to keep some pressure on that wound so it won't bleed so much. Keep an eye on his breathing and pulse too." She frowned. "Do you know CPR?" If his heart stopped...God, she didn't want to think like that.

Chester lifted an indignant eyebrow. "I may look and talk like a country bumpkin, but I know how to do that stuff. Learned it from the coast guard when I volunteered to help them on the weekends back in the eighties."

Blue smiled, chagrined. "Chester, you're one amazing guy."

His face flushed. "Well, I try."

Blue stood back out of the way as Chester maneuvered the sedan back onto the road. As soon as he was off, she climbed back into the truck. She didn't want to leave Drake alone any longer than necessary.

As she drove back to the house, her lips started to tingle all over again as she thought about that kiss. She had no idea what had possessed him, maybe fear of never seeing each other again, but whatever it had been, the kiss was something she wouldn't soon forget.

She parked close to the house and surveyed the yard and the edge of the woods carefully as she moved toward the front door. She had to call Director Casey and get some help down here. Lucas was missing and badly wounded. Time was no longer on their side. As she unlocked the door she said a quick silent prayer for Lucas and Ramon.

They were her friends…men she respected. If either of them died…

She refused to think like that.

Contrary to her orders, Drake waited in the parlor. "Medflight should be landing any moment," he told her.

Relief made her weak. "Good. I need to call Casey."

"I've already called Edgar. He said he would inform Casey immediately. He also suggested that we fax some of the photos to Casey's office so they can identify the woman, although Edgar was relatively sure who she was."

Blue remembered that Lucas had said that Rothman was a personal friend of Casey's.

"Victoria Colby," Drake went on. "She runs an elite private investigations agency in Chicago. Edgar feared that she might be in danger as well."

Blue knew the Colby Agency. She'd worked the tail

end of a mission involving Lucas's niece, Piper Ryan, and the Colby Agency had been involved. Ric Martinez, the Colby agent assigned to the case, was pretty unforgettable, she recalled as well.

"He wants any pictures we can find of Lowell for identification purposes."

Another idea surfaced amid Blue's chaotic thoughts. "Do you have a professional quality scanner with really high dpi? A five megapixel or better digital camera?"

Drake shrugged. "Sure. Rothman insisted I have only the best for communication purposes."

A smile slid across Blue's face. "All we need is one fingerprint on a glass or mirror, anything where it would be visible. Mission Recovery's lab can download it from the Net and use it to track down the identity of this bastard."

An answering smile tilted Drake's lips. "You are good, Maggie Callahan."

She winked at him, knowing full well she was flirting. "That's what they tell me."

As she passed Lowell's room on the way to Drake's quarters she smiled again as her mind formed a single word:

Gotcha!

Chapter Eleven

Noah watched Blue pace the floor as she conversed with Director Casey. They had spent the better part of the day going through Lowell's room and getting a good latent print downloaded and forwarded via the Internet to the Mission Recovery lab. Casey had immediately sent two of his top Specialists, along with a member of Mission Recovery's Housekeeping Team named Maverick who was acting as Blue's new backup to the island. Though they hadn't conversed other than a brief greeting, Noah was pretty sure Maverick was former military. About forty and quite physically fit, the man had the military demeanor down pat. He was accustomed to taking charge and he did it well. In addition, Victoria Colby had sent two of her finest agents as support.

They now knew that Lowell Kline's real name was Errol Leberman. Noah still had a hard time believing he'd been fooled so thoroughly. But, incredibly, it was true. According to Blue's director, Leberman had once been the archenemy of James Colby, Victoria's late husband. Blaming Colby for the murder of his family, he had ultimately been responsible for James Colby's death. Leberman had then gone underground and had not been heard from again until a few months ago.

Some of Victoria Colby's people had gathered intel indicating Leberman was on the move once more. One of Victoria's agents, a Simon Ruhl, had flown to Atlanta around noon to look into the art agent Noah had employed at Lowell's—Leberman's—urging. The man was oddly missing in action. It would take time to discover the tie-in between him and Leberman, if there was one, and Noah had a sneaking suspicion that there was. In his estimation, Leberman had assumed the identity of Lowell Kline in order to avoid detection by the Colby Agency and to bide his time until he could lure Lucas Camp here. The real Lowell Kline was most likely dead.

Noah had no way of knowing how Leberman had discovered his situation and the ultimate connection to Lucas Camp through Edgar Rothman's friendship with Director Thomas Casey. He, however, agreed with Director Casey's conclusions. Leberman had likely found himself a mole on the inside. If that proved the case, it would take time to ferret out the mole as well. Right now, they didn't have time. The consensus was that Leberman's attack on Lucas was orchestrated to bait Victoria Colby.

None of this really had anything to do with Noah, it seemed. He was not foolish enough to believe that Bonner had learned his lesson and was a changed man. He would exact his revenge at some point in time, maybe tomorrow, maybe next year. But, as Noah had known all along, Bonner would not bother with warnings such as useless notes. He would merely strike. Just another reason Noah could never risk allowing anyone to get close to him. Any woman who cared for him would be a valuable mark for vengeance.

He glanced at the parlor's wall clock as the one in the entry hall counted the hour. One in the morning. Neither he nor Blue had gotten any more sleep. He doubted either of them would until Lucas was found. Ramon's condition was critical. The trajectory of the bullet had caused it to glance off his skull, which was extremely fortunate; however, the resulting fracture and accumulating blood clot had required emergency surgery. Having lost a significant amount of blood had increased the risk. According to Blue he was a strong man. She was certain he would pull through.

Noah didn't want to consider how much blood Lucas had lost by now or what condition he was in. At fifty, maybe fifty-five, he was no longer a young man. Again, Blue insisted that there was not a tougher man alive than Lucas Camp. If anyone could pull through this, he could. Noah desperately hoped so. He could see in her eyes how much Lucas meant to her. Beyond basic human compassion for the man who was a stranger to him, Noah hoped he survived so that Blue didn't suffer that loss.

She ended the telephone conversation and collapsed on the couch. "They're still canvassing the island, but haven't found anything." She shook her head. "The island's not that big. Why can't they find him?"

Noah leaned forward and braced his elbows on his widespread knees. "There are many places to hide. Besides, Leberman could have taken Lucas off the island."

She forked her fingers through her hair and massaged the back of her head. "And where the hell did he go? He left the sedan. He had to have help. Disappearing on foot with a wounded man incapable of walking would be impossible.''

''A good strategist always plans for every contingency. He may have had other thugs at his beck and call,'' Noah reminded her of what she surely knew. She was weary with fatigue and worry, not thinking clearly. ''Why don't you get some more sleep? I'll be right here.'' He leaned back in his chair. ''Maverick's around here someplace. We'll keep watch.''

She shook her head, then stood. ''I couldn't sleep if I tried. I should make rounds. Check the locks.'' She straightened the shoulder holster she wore and suggested, ''You could scan the monitor.'' When he made no move to follow her directions, that blue gaze that reminded him so much of his ocean collided with his and she added, ''Drake, it's—''

''Noah,'' he corrected. ''It's past time you stopped calling me Drake.'' He stood and moved purposely toward her.

''Noah,'' she conceded, ''We have to—''

The telephone rang. Since the cordless receiver lay on the table next to the sofa, Blue answered it, no doubt grateful for the reprieve. There were things they needed to talk about, but, he supposed, now wasn't the time. Yet, the words burned inside him. Another time, he promised her silently as he watched the changing expressions on her face.

She listened to the caller for several seconds before saying, ''We'd have to find transportation.'' She frowned. ''I understand. Yes, sir.'' She depressed the Disconnect button.

''What now?'' Noah almost hated to ask.

''Apparently Victoria Colby received a telephone call a couple of hours ago indicating that Lucas had been found and that she should come to St. Gabriel right away.''

''It was Leberman,'' Noah guessed.

She nodded. ''Her second in command, Ian Michaels, has been trying to contact her for the past half hour to let her know that it's a setup, but she's already left the agency's private plane and apparently the call isn't getting through to her cell phone.''

''Wasn't someone keeping her office informed?'' Noah knew that the agency had already been advised of the possible threat to her.

''She received the call at home and no one knew she'd gone until about an hour ago. She gave the agent stationed at her house the slip.''

Noah quirked an eyebrow. ''She sounds a lot like you.''

Blue placed the telephone handset back in its base. ''She sounds a lot like she's headed for trouble. Casey wants me to head her off at the marina in Savannah. He doesn't want her on this island. Ian Michaels contacted Simon Ruhl in Atlanta. He's en route to Savannah to act as her personal security guard. I'll contact Maverick and have him take over here.''

Noah shook his head. ''No way. You're not going without me,'' he told her flatly. ''Either let Maverick go or I go with you.''

''There's no time to discuss the issue, Noah,'' she insisted. Despite his irritation and the situation, the sound of his name on her lips made him yearn to hear it again. ''Casey ordered me to go. I can't risk having her arrive here and...''

''Then let's not argue. I'm going with you.'' He took her by the arm and headed toward the front door. ''Besides, you wouldn't know where to go for transportation to the mainland anyway. You'll need me for that."

Well, he had her there, Blue admitted silently. "What if we can't get back in time? Have you even left the island in the past five years?"

That dark gaze settled onto hers, the finality there unmistakable. "We'll be back in time."

By 3:00 a.m. Blue was edging toward panic.

"You're certain the message I received was a hoax?" Victoria Colby asked for the third time.

"Yes, ma'am," Blue explained yet again. "We believe Leberman is trying to lure you to the island using Mr. Camp as bait."

The look of distress that marred the woman's face revealed clearly the depth of her feelings for Lucas.

She shook her head. "I should have killed Leberman when I had the chance."

Blue's gaze met Noah's. To say that the statement surprised her would be putting it mildly. One never expected that kind of thing from a lady dressed in designer clothes and with the presence and carriage of a highbrow sophisticate.

"Ma'am, I'm sure Mr. Ruhl will be here soon and he'll explain everything more completely."

Blue glanced at the sky once more, then back at Noah. He didn't look at all concerned, but she damn sure was. Every minute they waited put them that much closer to dawn. The boat ride back to St. Gabriel was a good thirty minutes. This was just too close for comfort.

Mr. Venable, grumping about the ungodly hour with every breath since they'd rousted him from bed, waited in the boat. Blue had insisted that Mrs. Colby remain in the limo with her pilot and the driver. She and Noah did the same.

To her extreme relief a car at last pulled into the parking area. The pilot, who sat in the passenger seat next to the driver, checked his side mirror. "It's Simon."

Blue breathed easy for the first time since leaving the house. She had to get Noah back there. She and Noah emerged from the car and greeted the arriving agent. He was tall. Definitely the dark, silent type.

Before Blue could stop her, Victoria got out as well.

"Victoria," Simon said with an acknowledging nod. "You had us scared there for a little while."

She shook her head. "I'm certain it was Lucas's voice."

Blue remained silent, as did Noah, and allowed her agent to allay her concerns.

"It may very well have been his voice, but that doesn't mean it was on the up-and-up. You'll be safer here in Savannah. Miss Callahan and her people will keep us informed." He looked to Blue.

"Of course," Blue agreed. "You'll know the minute we hear anything."

Victoria reluctantly gave in. "All right. We'll wait." She glanced at Blue, then Noah. "Thank you for coming." She blinked furiously at the tears welling in her eyes. "I apologize for the inconvenience."

Noah gifted her with one of his rare, charming smiles. "It was no inconvenience whatsoever, Mrs. Colby."

She managed a semblance of a smile. "Have a safe trip back to the island. And find Lucas, would you?"

Getting back to the island and then the house could be a little tricky, however, the promise they made to

Victoria Colby about finding Lucas might just prove impossible.

Leberman could be waiting near the island dock. Victoria's instructions had been wait at the dock once she arrived, for transportation on the island. He could have more underlings like the two they'd taken down after Lucas's shooting watching from just about anywhere on the island.

But she and Noah had no choice. It was a risk they had to take.

Noah's life depended upon getting back to the house before daybreak.

THE PINK HUES of a distant dawn were streaking across the sky by the time they reached the house. Noah's hands shook when he attempted to unlock the door, his only visible concession to the anxiety hurtling through them both. Blue sensed his urgency, and very nearly had a nervous breakdown herself. She was certain Mr. Venable would refuse any future offer, no matter how generous, to take her or Noah anywhere. The tension had been as thick as peanut butter during the race across the expanse of water that separated St. Gabriel from the mainland.

Her stomach still churned from the rocky journey.

As soon as the door was locked behind them and the code entered into the security keypad, they performed a quick search of the house. Noah had started arming the security system since Lowell—Leberman—had never been privy to the code. Blue put in a call to Director Casey that the mission had been accomplished. He was greatly relieved. Whatever fate lay in store for Lucas, he would not want any harm to come to Victoria. Blue was positive of that as well.

As she and Noah collapsed on the sofa in the parlor, she wondered what it would feel like to know that kind of love.

Unbidden her gaze moved to Noah. He looked tired. She was certain he'd had even less sleep than she had. She thought again of what he'd told her about Rothman's suggestion that he try the antidote serum. She wished that Noah could have his life back...could walk out into the sunlight without fear. But he was right, trying the serum wasn't worth the risk.

She'd rather have him forever in the darkness than lose him entirely.

The thought gave her a start. What was she thinking? He didn't belong to her in any sense of the word. When this mission was over she would leave, even if she did linger for that unfinished business. Their lives were destined for different courses. But each time she looked at him, as she did now, she realized how accurately she had imagined the artist behind the painting. He was everything she'd fantasized he would be.

"If only I could read your mind," he said softly, his voice silky, dangerous. Dangerous to her heart.

She inclined her head and studied him. "I'm exhausted. If you could read my mind, you'd..." She sighed then. "You'd know that I feel helpless. I can't do anything for Lucas...I..." She shook her head.

"You need sleep."

She shook her head again, then her newly determined gaze settled on his. "There are things we need to talk about. Like your artwork. I want the truth about Noah Drake."

Tension reverberated inside him, but he tamped down the automatic response. He could share his love of painting with her. Not only could he, he wanted to.

How smart was that? He almost laughed at his continued need to protect himself. What did it matter anyway? She would be gone soon...it was too late to change the fact that he had grown attached to her. Why pretend? Why ignore the need that would not be slaked by any other means but touching her...having her.

"The truth?" he asked.

She nodded and relaxed more fully into the leather cushions.

"I received my first canvas and set of oil paints as a gift from my mother on my twelfth birthday. She was an artist and I was pretty good as a kid. At least she thought so." He hadn't thought of his parents in so long the concept of having family hardly felt real. The memories were almost like someone else's! He'd trained himself not to think of them. It was easier that way. No, it was more than simply easy, it was necessary.

"Where are your parents now?" she asked, obviously sensing his melancholy.

"They died in a house fire about ten years ago while I was away on a mission. They were buried long before I even knew they were dead." He would always regret that. He'd been an only child; there had been no one else. A longtime family friend had taken care of the arrangements and pushed the Department of Defense until they located Noah.

"So you started to paint seriously when you were twelve?" she prodded him back to the subject at hand.

He nodded. "But as time went on one thing or the other always got in the way. Girls, cars." More recollections he hadn't considered in years. "After signing on with the military I never looked back." He

glanced around the parlor, considered that this place
had been his prison for five years now and yet he'd
never really *lived* here. He'd merely existed, gleaning
minute fragments of happiness from his ocean and his
painting.

"When *this* happened, I had nothing and no one.
Finally I turned to the one thing I'd always wanted to
do…painting." He shrugged self-consciously. "It's
kept me sane…" He thought about the waves crashing
against the sand outside and even the house that he
more often referred to as a prison than not. All of it,
even the island had kept him grounded to a certain
extent. Yes, the bitterness was still there, but it had
lessened somehow these past few days.

She was the reason.

For the first time in five long years he felt something
more than the bitterness…more than the need to paint
and to run in the darkness. He felt desire and physical
need. And those emotions were reciprocated, he knew.
Whether she permitted herself to admit the truth or
ever allowed herself to succumb to the temptation, she
was drawn to him. That simple, basal response awakened his long-slumbering libido.

"Well—" she curled her legs under her "—if we're
going to play truth or dare here, I suppose I can con-
fess my secret as well."

Anticipation burned through him. This he wanted to
hear. He'd thought he knew everything there was to
know about Maggie "Blue" Callahan. Maybe he
didn't have such a big head start in the knowing game
after all.

"I'm intrigued," he said, stretching his legs out in
front of him for comfort. "Don't keep me in sus-

pense.'' Getting her mind off Lucas would help her relax, if only for a few minutes.

Her gaze traveled the length of him, then moved on to other things around the room as if looking directly at him as she spoke was too difficult. ''About six months ago I was in a little Georgetown gallery and I discovered this wonderful painting.'' She closed her eyes as if imagining the work. The smile told him that it was a pleasant memory…one that she relished recalling. When she at last opened her eyes, she continued, ''I'd always assumed that I was above becoming obsessed with anything other than my work.'' She laughed softly. ''Boy, was I wrong. The scene drew me in, kept me entranced for hours on end. I just couldn't get enough of looking at it.''

A new kind of tension moved through him, sending his heart into a faster rhythm…making his pulse react.

''I found myself imagining all kinds of things about the man who'd painted that haunting forest scene. It had to be a man—or maybe I just wanted to believe that. He had to be dark, of course, to convey that enigmatic mood…the forbidden sense of sensuality.'' Her gaze shifted to his and those blue eyes glittered with unconcealed lust. ''I was right. It was you. *N.D.D.*''

He needed to touch her, but he didn't dare break the spell. The air was charged with their mutual desire, edged with the raw tension of recent events. His loins tightened with the need pooling there.

She turned away for a long moment. He was afraid she might not say any more, and he so wanted to hear the rest. Finally, she allowed him to see her eyes again.

''I felt it the moment I arrived on the island. A sense of familiarity…of knowing. And then, when we met,

I knew there was a connection there, something that drew me to you other than that handsome face and made-for-sin body.''

A smile crept across his lips. ''Made-for-sin body?''

She shrugged. ''I did see you in that towel, you know.''

He nodded. ''Ah, yes, you did.''

''*Sin* would definitely be the right word.''

He splayed his hands and shook his head. ''I wish I could claim some special connection that made me notice you, but I can't.'' The uncertainty in her eyes told him she didn't know how to take his admission. ''I simply wanted you the moment I saw you. No pomp and circumstance, just plain old lust.''

She blushed becomingly, the dusky red making the rest of her skin look even creamier. ''I see. So you didn't want a bodyguard, you just wanted a body.''

''Not just any body,'' he pointed out. ''Your body.''

Her pulse skipped at the confession. Warmth spread through her immediately just sitting there looking at him. He wanted her…she wanted him. Time to find a distraction.

''I think I'll hit the shower.'' She stood, stretched and sighed. ''You okay for a few minutes?''

He had her .38, not to mention a gun cabinet filled with weapons. She didn't have to ask if he knew how to use them. He was ex-military, not Special Forces but something on that order.

He nodded, saying nothing as she hurried up the stairs without looking back. If she'd looked back she was certain he would have seen the invitation to join her in her eyes.

That would not be conducive to keeping her distance emotionally. Definitely not a good thing.

Well, she was certain it would be good, physically anyway, but it wasn't the right choice.

In her room, Blue shucked her clothes. She turned on the shower and checked the soap, a new habit she'd acquired since coming here. She glanced at her reflection in the mirror, noting the bruises and healing scratches from the glass slivers. She wondered what Noah saw when he looked at her. Did he feel the depth of emotion she felt when she looked at him? Or was it still just plain old lust? She wanted to believe he felt more now. She shouldn't allow herself to go there. She couldn't fall in love with this man. But, if she was honest with herself, she was halfway there already.

Incredibly bad timing for both of them.

She stepped beneath the warm spray and allowed the water to sluice over her. Slowly her muscles relaxed and she sighed with gratitude. Her thoughts went to Lucas and she wanted to cry. She prayed fervently that God would keep him alive and that they would find him. She thought of the worry in Victoria Colby's eyes. Blue knew then and there that if Noah was wounded and missing, she'd feel much the same way.

"Idiot," she muttered. It wasn't smart to fall in love with a man she could never have...who wanted nothing from her but a physical relationship. Her mother had always warned her that sex without commitment was trouble. An old-fashioned concept, but regrettably true in most cases. In this one without doubt.

For the first time in longer than she could remember, Blue felt homesick. She wished she could hug her mother and kick back with her dad and have a beer. She even missed her brothers. Now that was saying something.

The tears came unbidden and without warning.

Once they started she seemed to have no control over them whatsoever. She pressed her forehead to the slick tile and sobbed as quietly as she could. What was wrong with her? She never cried.

The metal-on-metal slide of the shower door brought her head up. Her eyes widened as she took in the naked Adonis standing before her in all his glory. Her breath evaporated in her lungs. Before she could find her voice, Noah stepped in next to her. He pressed a gentle kiss to her forehead, then wrapped those strong arms around her. She told herself to resist, but she simply couldn't.

It felt so good to be held by him. The warmth and sinew of his body made her feel safe and at home. How could she even think of pushing him away? She closed her eyes and inhaled deeply the scent of his masculine skin, resisting the impulse to burrow her face into that awesome chest. He whispered soothing words to her, his voice so soft. By contrast, his body was hard, yet welcoming. She could feel every perfect contour...every amazing plane of hot male flesh. Her heart plummeted, landing somewhere in the vicinity of her tummy and then surged upward again and thundered back to life. Her skin tingled with the caress of his. She wanted to touch him everywhere at once, but for now she was content just to hold him, to have him hold her.

And then he kissed her and all else ceased to matter.

Those full, wonderfully carved lips moved down to cover hers more completely. He angled her head for better access and her lips parted of their own volition. His hot, steamy tongue thrust into her mouth, making her whimper with need. Her whole body throbbed with that same need. Instinctively she arched into his generous, fully aroused sex.

There was no denying that he wanted her, was more than ready to take her, but he held back, took his time.

Slowly, tenderly, he washed every inch of her body. Kissed every scratch and bruise. By the time he'd shampooed her hair, she was clutching at the slick walls and perched on the edge of climax. Battling for control, she returned the favor, hoping to push him to the edge while slowing her plunge toward it, all the while reveling in the marvelous textures of his body. The smooth taut skin…the dark, wiry body hair. Ridges and planes of pure, honed muscle…the velvety smoothness and arousing thickness of his sex. She wanted him inside her now!

She kissed that carnal mouth and moaned at the sweetness of his taste. "I don't think I'll live another minute if you—"

He shut off the cooling water and stepped out of the shower, bringing her with him. Taking his time he dried her body with the towel she'd placed on the sink. Then he kissed her again and she rubbed down his sleek body with that same towel. His kiss was urgent as their lips met once more, impatient almost. He was nearing that same precipice where she clung precariously. A thrill went through her at the thought that she could take him to that place. He'd been so distant…so remote and untouchable at first.

The man lifting her into his arms and carrying her to the bed was far from untouchable and remote. He was giving and tender, greedy and savage. And she wanted more.

As if their minds were linked, he settled between her thighs, not wasting time on more foreplay. She was ready for him...ready to take all that he would give her. And she knew he was ready too.

He lifted her bottom with strong, sure hands, nudged her entrance. Sweet sounds of urgency and need echoed around them, his guttural, primal, hers more high-pitched but equally desperate. Slowly, he sank into her, the delicious sensation of penetration very nearly unbearable.

Her palms flattened against his chest, she felt the beating of his heart and his name slipped past her lips on a wispy breath. *Noah*. He kissed her painstakingly slowly, the deep, stretching thrusts of his lovemaking equally unhurried. His body keeping a perfect tempo with that skilled mouth.

Time stood still as they climbed higher and higher together, their bodies reaching...aching for release. And when it came it was mind-blowing...with frantic words and kisses...with fingers fisted in the tangled sheets and clutching sweat-dampened skin.

When he at last lay beside her, she tried to think of the right words to say, but nothing felt right enough. A contented sigh drifted from her lips and he kissed her again.

"I wish I could see you in the light of day," she whispered without thought, then realized her mistake. "I'm sorry. I meant that I want to know every detail of your face."

He turned toward her and took her hand in his then kissed her palm. "I understand." He placed that same hand against his jaw. "There are other ways to see a person."

Understanding what he meant, she reached up with her other hand, wondering why she hadn't thought of that herself. She examined every hollow and ridge...every line and angle. She traced the balanced perfection of his nose, then his slightly heavy brow and those chiseled jaws, that square chin. By the time she'd had her fill of touching his face, her body was fully aroused all over again.

As was his.

His lips found hers, teasing, tasting. "I need to make love to you again," he murmured, his voice husky with desire, then he stilled. "I *want* to make love to you."

The distinction he made sent her foolish heart rejoicing. Desperate to regain some form of control, she urged him onto his back and moved onto all fours over him. "Only if I can be on top this time," she teased brushing her torso along the length of his.

The scream of an alarm shattered the moment.

Blue reared up, Noah came up with her. "Is that—?" Her first thought was that someone had entered the house...Leberman.

"Smoke detectors," he said.

They were out of the bed and dragging on clothes before the words were fully out of his mouth.

Blue grabbed her Glock and followed Noah into the hall.

The smoke was so thick she could scarcely see him right in front of her.

She looked both ways down the hall—nothing but smoke. It boiled up from the staircase.

Fear banded around her chest.

The house was on fire.

Chapter Twelve

Noah moved down the staircase as quickly as he dared. Touch was his only guide.

Smoke hung as thick in the air as any fog he'd ever seen. There was no time to try and determine where the fire had started or where it was headed. He considered briefly the tunnel exit, but it was fraught with crumbling steps and decaying walls.

He had to get Blue to safety *now*.

His lungs burned with the acrid smell. Behind him Blue coughed hard. They had to hurry.

Reaching the front door, he grabbed the knob and started to turn the lock.

Blue pushed between him and the door, knocking his hands free of the lock.

"The sun is rising," she stammered between bouts of coughing. "You can't—"

"There's no choice." He set her aside and opened the door.

"Noah, stop!"

The security alarm activated and sounded its siren.

Ignoring her plea as well as the wailing of the security system, he rushed outside, dragging her with him. Smoke rolled out behind them.

For several seconds he froze, blinked and tried to see through the gray mist swirling around them, enveloping them like a cocoon.

He was outside.

It was not dark.

Move—no time to think.

He propelled Blue down the steps.

As they rushed across the yard toward the edge of the woods, putting distance between them and the smoke…the danger, the sun peeked above the horizon.

Long, glowing streaks of light reached across the blue water…across the sand, spilling over all in its path, including Noah.

The first strike of pain was like a bullet to his brain. He staggered. Blinked.

A shower of agony erupted in his head and spiraled down the length of his body, paralyzing him on the spot.

"Keep going!"

Blue pushed him forward…toward the shelter of the trees.

His movements were pure survival instinct urged on by the woman beside him. He couldn't think… couldn't process the necessary actions required to reach safety.

The pain undulated beneath his skin…sizzled and crackled like a slowly building fire. Breathing grew difficult. His heart raced harder, faster as if attempting to outrun the misery blazing along his nerve endings.

They reached the trees. His knees buckled. He couldn't go any further. His eyes refused to remain open…the pounding in his head grew louder, more insistent.

"You can't stop now!" She pulled at him, trying

to get him back to his feet. "Noah! You have to move."

"What the hell happened?"

A male voice.

Maverick.

"Help me get him to the old chapel. It's that way...I think. Hurry, Maverick. It's the light. He can't be in the light."

Fear was in her voice. She was afraid for him.

Noah felt only the pain...the need to surrender to the blackness swooped down on him like a hawk, talons ready for the kill.

The voices around him were distant blurs of sound now. He felt himself being lifted and dragged forward. An anguished groan echoed around him. He realized belatedly that it must have come from him for he felt it more than heard it. Awareness faded to nothing.

BLUE AND MAVERICK stumbled into the old chapel, dragging Noah between them. It was almost pitch-dark in the farthest corners of the rickety building and that's where they headed. She could scarcely draw a breath for the thundering in her chest. *God, please don't let him die,* she prayed.

"Here," she told Maverick. Together they lowered Noah to the floor.

"He's not dead," Maverick told her, after checking for a pulse. "Do we need a medflight?"

She shoved a handful of hair behind her ear and tried to think. "Use your cell phone. Call Rothman. Find out what to do. I'll stay with him."

"Will do." Maverick moved toward the front of the decaying structure. "I guess I'll check on the house, call the fire department too."

Blue nodded, not caring if he saw her or not, tears streamed down her cheeks. "Close the doors, Maverick. We need the darkness."

"Hang in there, Blue, I'll get help." His deep voice was full of reassurance, but she knew even Maverick couldn't fix this problem.

The doors closed, leaving them in total darkness.

For the first time in her life, Blue was not afraid of the dark. She was too damned scared that Noah was dying to be afraid of anything else.

The sounds he made in his suffering wrenched her heart. There was nothing she could do. She held his hand and prayed for help. His skin was like ice. A sob twisted through her. If help didn't come soon—

"Step out of the way."

The seemingly disembodied voice came out of the darkness maybe a half dozen feet away.

Female.

Vaguely familiar.

Blue leaned back on her heels and simultaneously reached for the Glock in her waistband at the small of her back.

"You won't be needing that," the voice cautioned.

The old woman from that first night in the woods.

Blue didn't have to see her to know for sure. The distinct sound of her voice poked through the numerous layers of fear and anxiety pressing down on Blue. She thought of the voodoo doll. Leberman had put it there when he drugged her. An attempt to frighten her. The old woman was dead, he'd claimed. But here she was.

"What are you doing in—?"

"Makes no nevermind about that." The old woman

knelt next to Noah. "Now move aside before you be the death of him."

Blue obeyed. "It's the light," she started to explain. "He can't—"

"I know what ails him. Now leave us so I can mend him."

Not in this lifetime, lady. "I won't leave him."

The woman turned toward her. Though it was dark as tar in the old chapel, Blue could see her eyes…her expression as if some sort of inner glow suddenly made her visible. Or maybe her own eyes had simply adjusted to the lack of light. The long slashing scar stood out in stark relief against the woman's mahogany skin.

"This has to be done in private…between me and him only. If you stay, I can't help him and he'll die."

A new rush of tears bloomed in Blue's eyes. She tried to think this through, tried to reason, but there was no rationale for what was happening. She could feel the old woman's energy. Her gut told her to listen and believe…to take that leap of faith. But her heart pleaded with her to stay right beside him.

"Okay." She looked the old woman dead in the eyes. "Don't you let him die. You'll have to answer to me if you do."

She nodded her understanding. "Wait outside, Maggie Callahan. And watch your back. Evil is very close."

A chill raced up her spine, almost paralyzing her, but Blue forced herself to move. She kissed Noah's hand, then laid it at his side and followed the old woman's orders without looking back. Once outside she closed the doors behind her.

She told herself that she'd prayed for help and the

old woman had suddenly appeared. Blue didn't believe in that voodoo mumbo-jumbo...or so she'd thought. Right now she wasn't sure what she believed. She only knew that Noah was dying. She felt that reality with every fiber of her being.

And she couldn't bear it.

Blue collapsed onto the dilapidated steps, braced her arms on her knees and buried her face there. She wept like a child, uncontrollably and openly for a full minute before she pulled it back together.

She pushed to her feet and swiped the moisture from her cheeks. She had a job to do.

Parting the deep weeds she moved to the rear of the old chapel and listened intently. An ache pierced her at the sound of Noah's soft groans. The low chanting of the old woman was a perpetual hum underscoring the sounds of his suffering.

Forcing her personal feelings aside, Blue did the only thing she could, she squared her shoulders and assumed a posture and position to keep watch over the chapel.

And then she prayed some more.

BY NOON the sounds inside the old chapel had ceased. Blue wanted to bang on the wall and call out to the old woman, but she didn't. If Noah was resting she didn't want to disturb him. From the look of the place, a strong wind could take it down. She wasn't about to risk making the wrong move.

Maverick had checked in with her a few times and had things under control at the house.

Blue kept a watchful vigil knowing that forcing Noah out of the house could have been a move by General Bonner to render him vulnerable. For that matter, Leberman could want him dead. Though she couldn't see the motive in that, psychos didn't always have a rational motive. Maverick had put down perimeter alarms in the area to assist her. If anyone crossed the invisible laser beam, she would know it, but the intruder would not.

He had also left a field-op communications set with her to keep a link between them in case she needed backup in a hurry, and for hearing the alarm if the perimeter was breached. A distinct tone would sound in her earpiece. She'd pinned the tiny transmitter to her neckline, and snugged the earpiece into place. A single stroke of her finger would activate the transmitter for a direct link to Maverick and vice versa.

It took every ounce of willpower she possessed not to dwell on Noah's condition or the lovemaking they'd shared only hours ago. The way he'd kissed her every injury, his whispered words of need and desire, made her ache inside for his touch. Her heart reacted instantly to the memories. He'd made love to her with an urgency that had been at once incredibly intense and beautifully tender. His strength and control was all that had kept the sweet joining from becoming a frantic act of desperation.

She thought of the depth of emotion it took to create those masterful works of art she'd seen in his secret room, emotion he consciously denied for fear of losing control. She recognized the battle, it was far too familiar. She fought that same war, had done so since the moment she'd first laid eyes on his painting in that Georgetown gallery. Meeting the man had simply been the proverbial straw that broke the camel's back.

Unable to help herself, she touched the wall closest to where she'd left Noah. The wood was soft with age and covered with ivy and resurrection fern. She wished again that she could see inside…could know that he was alive and no longer suffering so horribly.

"Blue Bell, how's it going out there?" Maverick's voice sounded in her earpiece.

Despite her current state of emotions she almost laughed. No one, absolutely no one, not even her brothers, dared call her Blue Bell. Only Maverick.

"Too quiet," she said bleakly. "I don't know how much longer I can take the not knowing."

Maverick made a tsking sound. "I don't know what I'm going to do with you young folks. I swear, if it's not Logan or Ferrelli, it's you. We don't send you on assignment to fall in love. With the record you guys have been setting, we might as well start calling this unit Mission Cupid instead of Mission Recovery."

"What's up, Maverick?" she demanded grumpily. She had a good mind to tell him that if he had half a heart, he'd be doing the same damned thing. She couldn't help wondering what kind of love life the ruggedly handsome older man had. Just a touch of gray peppered his dark hair. She imagined he had his share of lady friends. Even at forty he was every bit as physically fit as his younger counterparts.

"The fire marshal has finished his walk through, but I didn't need him to tell me that we'd been had."

Maverick had called her within an hour of his going back to the house this morning and informed her that there hadn't been any fire. Smoke bombs strategically placed throughout the house had created the illusion. If Leberman was behind this and he had caused permanent damage to Noah…she was going to kill him herself. Too bad she couldn't kill him twice—once for Noah and a second time for Lucas.

Fury whipped through her anew. "You didn't find anything?" She had hoped that Leberman would leave some sort of clue, like the notes he'd obviously sent to Noah. But then, those had been nothing but a distraction...a ruse...bait to attract the real prey. She did wonder though how he had known Rothman would call Mission Recovery.

"*Nada.* What's more, the sheriff never received any calls about gunshots or intruders."

No surprise there. Sykes and Jaymo had been working for Leberman all along. Blue massaged the ache beginning in her forehead and wondered if Lucas was even still alive. She thought of Victoria Colby and what she must be going through as each hour passed with no news.

"Why the hell did he do this?" Dammit! What kind of games was he playing? What did he hope to accomplish?

"I wish I could tell you. I've opened all the windows and doors to air the place out. On the third floor there's some first-rate locks."

"That's Noah's suite," she said absently, her mind still searching for angles that somehow tied the latest stunt to draw out Noah to whatever Leberman had planned for Lucas and Victoria. "Security's topnotch."

"Good. You'll be safe there. I'm coming out there to relieve you."

"No way. I'm not leaving him."

"There's nothing you can do," Maverick said sternly. "You can't risk opening the door with the sun so bright right now. Rothman said that the darkness was his only hope of surviving. You need some downtime, Blue, or you'll be no good to him when night comes. Rothman said that you can't risk bringing him out in the daylight. There's nothing more to be done right now. He's on his way here."

"I can't leave...I..." He was right. She was exhausted. If she didn't get some sleep she'd be no good to anybody in a few more hours.

"Just for a couple hours, Blue. I'll give you a wake-up call before dusk. You'll be there to open the doors the moment darkness falls. Besides, you'll need to show Rothman the way to the chapel."

She exhaled a weary breath. It was the right thing to do, she knew. She pressed her ear to the wall and listened intently. Nothing. Noah would need her when night came. Preparation was half the game. She damn sure didn't want to fail him by being unprepared.

"All right. But just for a couple of hours."

"I'm on my way."

"Maverick," she said, a part of her still reluctant to leave Noah, "if anything—"

"Nobody's getting past me, girl," he interrupted, his tone a warning rather than a reassurance. "I started doing this when you were barely out of diapers. No one gets over on the Maverick."

Blue had to laugh. With the tension so high, if she hadn't laughed she would surely have cried. "You're right. What was I thinking?"

"Not with your head, that's for sure."

She accepted the dressing down without offense, she'd asked for that one. Rafe "Maverick" Scott had learned the personal protection and spy trade from the master—Lucas Camp.

BLUE AWOKE with a start. Her breath caught sharply as she sat straight up in bed. She blinked, startled all over again at the brightness of the room. The shutters and drapes were open. Fading sunlight spilled across the wine-colored carpeting. A moment passed before she gained her bearings.

Noah's room. Maverick had insisted that she stay in this room since it was the most secure.

Noah's bed.

Her heart hurtling into Fast Forward, she checked the clock on the bedside table. Still a good hour before sundown. The breath that had stalled in her lungs seeped past her lips. Thank God. For a second there she'd thought Maverick had let her oversleep.

Noah...her chest constricted as awareness flooded her, reminding her that he was hurt...maybe worse. And Lucas was still missing, his situation the same.

She picked up Noah's pillow and inhaled deeply of his scent. Though a hint of smoke still hung in the air as well as in the linens, she could smell his essence and she longed to touch him. To be with him again. The idea that Leberman had planted those smoke bombs to mimic a fire and drive Noah from the house enraged her all over again.

Climbing from the bed, she made a mental note of all she had to do before dusk. Quick shower, close and lock all the windows and doors, then get back to the old chapel.

She had to move fast.

The shower took five minutes, dressing a few more. She decided after a thorough toweling that her hair could air dry. Starting in Noah's room, she checked to ensure that all was as it should be and she methodically closed and locked all the windows Maverick had opened to let out the smoke, careful to shut the shutters and drapes as well.

With twenty minutes to spare, she scanned the front yard through the viewfinder and emerged from the house. Rothman had called and said that his flight had been delayed but that he would be here as soon as possible. Blue didn't like it, but there was nothing she could do about it. After locking the door she was halfway down the steps when Chester's truck arrived.

Simon Ruhl jumped from the bed of the truck. He opened the passenger-side door and Victoria Colby emerged from the cab of the old, dilapidated vehicle.

A new kind of anxiety seared through Blue. She wasn't supposed to be here. Had something else happened?

Oh, God. They'd found Lucas.

The deep circles under the older woman's eyes and her grave expression sent Blue's pulse surging toward panic.

"Have they found Lucas?" she demanded as she strode toward the truck. Why hadn't someone notified her?

Simon did not look happy. Another bad sign.

"I tried to talk her out of this, Miss Callahan," he said. "But she's too stubborn. Maybe you can reason with her." His exasperation evidenced itself in his posture. Blue knew exactly what he was feeling. He didn't like Victoria being on this island. He knew it wasn't safe, and, yet, she was the boss. What choice did he have but to obey her directions?

"What's going on?" This question Blue directed at Victoria Colby.

"Leberman called me," she said, her voice surprisingly strong considering what her state of mind must surely be. "I'm to go *alone* to meet him. I don't have time to argue."

"I don't understand." Blue shook her head. "You're supposed to meet him here?"

"There's a place, walking distance from here." She gestured back to the road. "I'm to walk out to the main road, go left and keep walking until I reach the next lane to the right. At the end of it there will be an old fishing shack. He'll meet me there."

"If you go at all, you can't go alone," Blue protested, conscious of the time. Dusk was almost upon them, she had to get back to the old chapel…to Noah.

Victoria's gaze pinned her with finality. "I don't have a choice. I have to go *alone.*"

"That's insane." Blue waved her hands as if erasing the notion. "We call the team in and we do a wide perimeter surveillance. He'll never know we're there."

Victoria moved her head from side to side, her expression implacable. "If I don't go alone, he'll kill Lucas."

Chapter Thirteen

"You have to trust me on this one, Victoria," Blue said, her tone brooking no argument. "You can't do this alone. He'll kill Lucas anyway."

Victoria shook her head, tears trickling past her lashes. "I lost my husband to that animal, I can't—"

"You're not going to lose Lucas," Blue said, suddenly as sure of it as she'd ever been of anything in her entire life. "Now let's stop wasting time and do this."

For one long, heart-stopping moment, Blue was sure the strong-willed lady wasn't going to give in, but with an assenting nod, she caved.

"We'll do it your way." Her gaze leveled on Blue's. "But, if you're wrong…"

"I'm not wrong." Blue said the words with the same certainty she felt in her gut. Leberman was going to kill Lucas anyway if they didn't get to him first; he only waited to lure Victoria in, otherwise Lucas would be dead already. Blue would not let that happen. Unless it was too late and no one knew it yet.

"Simon," she said to the Colby agent who was clearly impressed with her powers of persuasion, "call in the search team. Tell them to come in one at a time and to wait until they have the darkness for cover. If Leberman's watching, I don't want him to know we're up to anything.''

''Doing that as we speak.'' Simon flipped open what was obviously a secure cell phone. Mission Recovery had similar ones. It was unusual to find private-sector security and investigations personnel so well equipped. The Colby Agency was obviously highly sophisticated.

It was too risky to leave Victoria and Simon at the house; Leberman had access and wasn't afraid to make a move there. There hadn't been time to call a locksmith to the house. Chester stayed behind and the rest of the group headed through the woods to the old chapel.

Blue pressed her hand to her chest, suddenly remembering that she didn't have her light stick. The darkness was descending rapidly, but it didn't scare her quite the way it used to. Or maybe she was simply so focused on finding Noah and Lucas safe that nothing else mattered at the moment.

Whatever the case, the dark was the least of her problems at the moment.

''Maverick,'' she said after touching the disk on the lapel of her blouse, ''we're on our way.''

''Roger,'' he responded.

Maverick was already aware of Victoria's presence. He'd checked in to see that Blue was up and about right in the middle of her pleas for Victoria to listen to reason. The fact that he'd heard no sounds inside the chapel only added to Blue's heightening anxiety. Behind her, Simon via his secure phone alerted the team consisting of other Specialists as well as other Colby agents to the plan. Maverick had given Casey the heads up. He didn't like the idea any better than Blue did, but like her, he was out of suggestions and they were all out of options.

Lucas's condition could very well be critical now...if he was even still alive.

Few remaining streaks of sunlight filtered through the thick forest canopy by the time they reached the clearing where the old dilapidated structure stood. Blue wasted no time, she walked straight to the double doors.

"I'm going in now." She glanced at Maverick. "That old woman in there just better hope—"

Maverick angled his head toward the door. "I haven't heard a peep. You sure she was still in there when I took over?"

"Positive. And the doors haven't opened since I closed them and left Noah and the old woman in there?"

"Nope." Maverick shrugged. "We'll keep an eye on things out here while you check it out."

As Blue tugged on the old reluctant doors, she heard Maverick introducing himself to Victoria and Simon. Blue hadn't even thought of that. Giving herself grace, she did have other, more pressing matters on her mind.

An unexpected burst of air swept over her, filling her nostrils with the smell of the dank darkness of the crumbling interior. A shiver chased up her spine.

Even with the doors open, the ancient tomb-like place was dark. She moved cautiously toward the rear corner where she'd left Noah. She squinted, watching intently for any kind of movement.

"Hello," she finally said, annoyed that the old woman hadn't shown herself or spoken. "I'm back."

Silence.

Then she heard it.

The unmistakable sound of deep, rhythmic breathing.

Noah.

She rushed to his side and knelt next to him. She touched him and his flesh was warm. Her heart leapt with gladness. Gently, she shook him. "Noah, try to open your eyes." She shook him again. The pattern of his breathing changed, indicating that he recognized her presence or at the very least was aware that someone was speaking to him, touching him.

He turned his face toward her and pushed up into a sitting position. "Where are we?"

Blue's relief was so profound she could scarcely speak. "The old chapel. Are you okay? Any pain?"

Pause. "No...I feel fine. Rested."

The old woman had stuck by her promise. Blue turned, attempting to see her in the other dark corner. "Where's she hiding?"

"Who?" Noah tried to get to his feet and staggered a bit.

Blue immediately reached for him. "The old voodoo woman. I left her in here with you. She said she knew what to do."

"I don't know anything about any old woman, I've been asleep the whole time...apparently."

"Just stand still for a moment."

Leaving Noah standing there, Blue searched the entire structure by touch. There were no side rooms or closets, just one large room. Any furnishings had long since been removed.

She found nothing.

"Everything all right in there?" Maverick called from the door.

Shaking her head, Blue said, "We're coming out." She looped Noah's arm around hers and moved toward the door with him.

"Maybe the old woman was a ghost," Noah suggested, a smile in his voice.

Well, Blue didn't believe in ghosts. The old woman had been real. She was certain of it. But, if the idea made Noah smile, she was all for it. She refused to consider the gust of air that had greeted her the moment she opened the doors.

"Maybe so," she allowed. And maybe she was. What did Blue know about ghosts or angels? Really, who was to say that the old woman hadn't been a guardian angel? Blue might not actually believe in the supernatural, but she could keep an open mind.

NOAH WAS SURPRISED to find his home undamaged. Blue and Maverick explained about the smoke bombs and the still mystifying motive behind them.

With every waking moment Noah felt his strength returning. In fact, he felt more rested than he had in a very long time. He tried to remember the pain, had a vague impression of the first blinding stabs in his brain, but for the most part he couldn't recall anything after he and Blue had escaped the smoke-filled house.

Voodoo, indeed, he mused, thankful to be alive.

Three of Blue's cohorts, including Maverick, and two more of the Colby Agency's investigators had rendezvoused at the house. Headed by John Logan, the group was planning their strategy for covering Victoria as she followed Leberman's latest invitation.

"We have five more minutes," Victoria reminded curtly.

Though she was clearly upset, ravaged by anguish

if he had his guess, Victoria Colby was a strong woman, one who stood her ground as well as any man he'd ever met.

"Let's do it," Logan announced. "Ferrelli, you're our scout. You go now." Chester had given explicit instructions about several routes to the abandoned fishing shack. "We'll be three minutes behind you."

Ferrelli gave Logan a two-fingered salute and headed out.

"Maverick, you and Simon take the left side of the road, keep about thirty meters between your positions and Mrs. Colby."

Simon Ruhl, a former FBI agent Noah learned, nodded. "I'll take point," he offered.

"After you," Maverick agreed. He and Simon left the house through the kitchen. They would enter the woods on the south side of the house and move to the road.

"Max," Logan said to the other man Victoria's agency had sent as support, "you and I will take the left side."

Max, Pierce Maxwell, former DEA and well-qualified for just this sort of mission, inclined his head in acknowledgment of the order. "I'll be right behind you."

Logan glanced at Blue. "You and Drake stay in the house. I don't want him out in the open. We don't need two principals to watch."

"Wait." Noah could help. He had an advantage that none of them had. "Let me go. I can be right beside Mrs. Colby and no one would know."

"No way," Logan said firmly. "It's bad enough she's going. You're definitely not. If we get trapped, we might not make it back before dawn."

Noah started to argue again, but Logan stopped him with an upraised hand. "Besides, Blue may need you here."

That was the deciding factor for Noah.

Logan looked at Simon then. "You done any night ops before?"

Simon smiled. "I've done my share of night surveillance."

Logan lifted an eyebrow, but it was difficult to tell if he was impressed or skeptical. "Forget everything you learned. I want you to keep to the edge of the road, just barely out of sight in the tree line." Logan nodded to the Kevlar vest Simon had yet to don. "You'll need that. I want Leberman to know you're there. He won't believe for a minute that we'd send her in alone. If he thinks he's spotted her backup and takes you out, he might just let his guard down."

Simon quickly shouldered into the vest. "Good strategy." He secured the vest. "I had no intention of letting her out of my sight anyway."

"I hate to rush you, gentlemen," Victoria urged. "But we're out of time."

Logan gestured for her to precede him. In the entry hall, he said, "Mrs. Colby, I'd like you to wait sixty seconds before you and Simon leave the house. That'll give the rest of us time to get into position."

"I don't want to be late," she insisted, a tremor in her voice.

Logan gave her a reassuring smile. "Mrs. Colby, don't worry. You're the guest of honor. Leberman's gone to all this trouble to bring you here. He won't start his party without you."

She blinked, then nodded.

Logan and Max left via the kitchen as the others

had done. Noah and Blue waited in the entry hall with Victoria and Simon.

"Be careful," Blue said in warning as they exited next.

Victoria looked back at her. "No matter what happens," she said, her tone very nearly savage, "don't let that monster off this island."

The door closed behind them and Blue locked it securely. She turned around and sagged against it, then closed her eyes and let go a heavy breath.

"What if Lucas is dead already?"

Noah moved toward her, reaching out, then taking her into his arms. The powerful, fulfilling sensation of holding her rushed through him, making his knees weak and his head spin just a little. A dozen flashes of memory—of those moments they'd spent making love—flickered past his mind's eye.

He could hold her like this forever. Wanted nothing more than to make love to her again…here…now.

He drew back from her and felt an ache deep in his chest.

"You've done all you can. Now you have to wait."

This morning's events had driven home his reality as nothing else could. He and Blue could never be together in the real sense of the word. Could never have a real relationship or a family. He was a permanent inmate in this brick-and-mortar prison. She was a vital woman who thrived in her work. He could never ask her to give up her life for him. He wouldn't ask.

She pulled him close again and hugged him tight, as if reading his mind and knowing that the "they" that could be had come up short in his estimations, as it probably already had in her own.

She would be hurt by his selfish need to have her if only for a few moments. He knew he should admit that he'd made a mistake and attempt to set it right, but he simply could not call what they had shared for such a short space in time anything other than what it was…perfect, beautiful.

He inhaled deeply, relishing her sweet scent and remotely noting the lingering odor of smoke.

Everything inside him stilled.

He drew back, the epiphany hitting him with the force of a physical blow. "The entry alarm…"

Blue frowned at the sudden tension she felt in him. "What about the alarm?" She'd no more uttered the question than she realized exactly what he meant. Noah had started arming the security system since Leberman had a key and they now knew he was the enemy. The alarm hadn't gone off when the intruder placed the smoke bombs…at least not until they'd run out of the house. Maverick'd had to disarm it the old-fashioned way—with a heavy object—to shut it up. The particular system Noah had wasn't connected to a local police department or even a monitoring service. It was only for making him aware of an intruder.

"I set it when we came inside, remember?"

She did remember. "Maybe he figured out the code."

Noah shook his head. "Wouldn't matter, I set it on instant alarm. There was no delay. If anyone had opened a door or window, the alarm would have sounded at least until it was deactivated. With the code."

"We were preoccupied," Blue suggested, still certain there must be a rational explanation.

"Trust me," he insisted, that dark gaze firm on hers,

"we'd have heard it. You remember how loud it was when we rushed out of the house without disarming it."

She did…sort of, but she'd been so worried about Noah that she hadn't paid a lot of attention to it. Still, he was right. They would have heard it.

She shrugged. "The smoke bombs weren't set on a timer. He had to have activated each one as he placed it. How'd he get in without tripping the alarm?"

A look of disbelief captured Noah's expression. "There's only one way, but no one was supposed to know about it except me."

"What way? How?" Anticipation spiked inside her.

"Call Logan," Noah ordered her. "Tell him it's a setup of some kind. Lucas won't be at the fishing shack."

Noah started to pull away from her. She held onto his arm. "Wait a minute. How do you know he isn't at the fishing shack?"

His gaze collided fully with hers once more. "Because I know where he is. Call the team back."

Anxiety welling in her, pressing down on her pounding heart, Blue activated her communicator. "Logan, do you copy?"

Noah walked to the wood-paneled area beneath the staircase. The place where most architects designed coat closets or small powder rooms to utilize what would otherwise be wasted space.

"We're almost in position," Logan said quietly. "Do you have an emergency?"

Blue hesitated, for one seemingly endless beat considering that what she was about to do might very well cost Lucas his life. Noah looked at her across the dimly lit expanse of wood flooring. And right before her eyes, a wide panel popped open revealing a hidden doorway.

"Logan, the mission is aborted! Do you copy? Be advised, it's a setup. You have to get Mrs. Colby away from there…back to the house, anywhere, but keep her away from that fishing shack. I repeat, abort your mission."

A tension-filled nanosecond passed.

"Standing down," Logan responded. "ETA to your destination, six minutes."

Noah waited at the open doorway for her to join him. "What is this?"

"I should have told you. At first I was too stubborn to let you in on it, and then…"

Blue looked past him, a winding stone staircase appeared to go down toward what she presumed to be a cellar. "Is it a basement?" Why would Leberman risk keeping Lucas that close by?

"It's my backup egress route. It leads down to a tunnel that comes out in one of the caves a couple of miles down the beach. Smugglers once used it. There's even a stolen treasure or two still hidden away down there."

"But what if Lucas isn't down there? What if Leberman just used it for access?"

Noah smiled. "He's down there. I even stored emergency supplies there in case I had to hide out for a few days. That's where he's been all this time."

Complete comprehension dawned on Blue. That's why the team hadn't been able to find him anywhere on the island and yet he was close enough to set the smoke bombs. He'd been right under their noses all along.

Evil is very close. The old woman's words made perfect sense now.

Noah's gaze turned serious. "I should go alone. Wait for Logan and the others and then you can follow."

"No way. I'm sticking to you like glue."

Something flitted through his gaze...something knowing and secretive. "You can try."

He started down the winding stairs. "Watch your step. It's dark down here and a lot of the steps are crumbling."

And then she knew what he had planned. He was going to disappear on her. Blue hurried to catch up with him. She would not let him get far enough ahead of her to lose her.

The stairs were narrow and uneven. The walls rough with time. More than once she lost her balance and had to brace against Noah to regain it. That old familiar fear of the dark edged into her consciousness. She pushed it away, but the panic would not be denied completely. She blinked, tried to force her eyes to adjust, but it was just too dark. The smell was suffocating...the air old, tainted with the wicked deeds of pirates and smugglers. A quiver rippled through her. She'd been listening to Chester too much.

Finally they reached the bottom step. The passage was nearly as narrow as the staircase had been. A musty odor, mingled with the scent of decayed fish and saltwater, hung in the thick air this far down. She ignored the claustrophobic sensation that tried to take root. She would not be afraid. Noah was with her. She had her Glock. And backup was on the way.

Noah stopped. She bumped into his muscular back. A sound echoed farther down the passage.

Moving more slowly…not making a single noise, they edged forward in unison.

The tunnel widened. Her fingers encountered dips in the walls, cave-like openings or adjoining passages.

Another of those low groans.

Louder…closer.

Five, maybe six more yards and they were nearly on top of the sound. A dim glow emanated from one of the side passages another six or seven yards ahead. Her heart kicked into a frantic rhythm. They moved more quickly now.

"Who's there?" a male voice asked gruffly.

Lucas.

Blue pushed past Noah, rushing toward the sound of Lucas's voice. He was lying on a military-style sleeping bag. Even in the dim light he looked like death warmed over. Pale, hollow-eyed.

Lucas manacled her wrist with surprising strength when she moved to inspect his wounds. "Where's Victoria?" he growled.

"Don't worry. She's with Logan and the others. We know the fishing shack is a setup. They're on their way back here."

His hold on Blue tightened. "Get her off this island. Now!" He coughed hard, then groaned with the pain the spasm caused.

"Callahan, do you copy?" echoed in her earpiece. Logan.

"Copy, Logan. We've found Lucas."

"We're back at the house. What's your twenty?"

"The door under the staircase. We're in the tunnel beneath the property. There's no sign of Leberman, but it isn't safe to bring Mrs. Colby down here."

Gunfire erupted at the end of the tunnel. A half

dozen lightning-fast flashes of light. Semi-automatic. Nine-millimeter, she estimated. A bullet whizzed past her head. Where was Noah?

Blue hunkered into a crouch, simultaneously pushing Lucas farther into the niche and then shielding him with her own body.

Blue assumed a firing position, but couldn't locate Noah. How could she fire when he could be anywhere?

More gunshots. Revolver. The .38.

Noah.

She hissed a curse. Dammit. He was going to get himself killed.

The next succession of rapid fire was farther away…the semi-automatic again.

"Douse that light, Callahan," Maverick's voice in her ear this time.

Railing at herself for not thinking to do that already, she leaned across Lucas and turned down the flame on the kerosene lantern until it went out. She blinked, forcing her eyes to adjust as quickly as possible. She felt more than heard the team as they moved past her position. Someone knelt beside her.

"Mr. Camp, I'm going to help Specialist Callahan get you out of here."

Simon Ruhl's voice.

The time it took to move Lucas was considerable. He was too weak to help in any way. Though Blue was intensely relieved that they'd found Lucas and he was very much alive, she couldn't help worrying about Noah and the rest of the team out there with Leberman. She told herself repeatedly as they moved up the stairs one agonizing step at a time that the men after Leberman were highly trained and more than capable.

But she kept remembering the way he'd fooled her…had fooled everyone. He was not an enemy to take lightly. He was the worst kind.

The kind you didn't see coming.

CHESTER MADE the necessary calls to have a medflight land right on the beach behind the house to take Lucas to the closest trauma center. Thank God one was available immediately. Victoria Colby, by sheer determination, was permitted to go with him. The allowance was a first in Blue's experience. But then she'd never met a woman like Victoria.

Simon and Maverick, who'd stayed with Victoria while the others went after Leberman, now waited with Blue. Unlike them, she paced the floor. None of the team members still on the hunt had communicated any information one way or the other. When a team went dark, meaning silent, then that move was respected by those waiting for word. No one dared take any risk of giving away their position.

Blue understood that rule as well as anyone, but she had a hell of a time sticking by it as the minutes and hours dragged by.

The clock in the entry hall struck the witching hour.

"Enough, Blue," Maverick said. "Sit down and stop that pacing."

The two men had taken up positions in the living room an hour or so ago, but Blue had continued to wear a path in the entry hall.

"I don't want to sit," she argued, annoyed that he didn't understand that.

His gaze softened. "I know what you're going through, but you've got to be reasonable. Now sit down." He gestured to the sofa.

She raked her fingers through her hair and expelled an exasperated breath. Lucas was safe. Victoria was safe. Noah wasn't out there alone. And the dark was certainly his ally. She supposed she should be thankful.

"We're coming in," Logan's voice suddenly echoed in her ear. "We lost him."

Blue looked from Maverick to Simon and back. They'd all heard the same thing.

Leberman had gotten away.

No team wanted to fail…but to know that kind of sick mind was on the loose made Blue nauseous. Without Leberman they would probably never find out who had helped him learn about Noah and his condition or Rothman's connection to Lucas. There would be at least one more unknown enemy…unless it was the general. And that was highly improbable.

An abrupt pounding on the front door jerked her attention in that direction.

Maverick and Simon were next to her in a heartbeat, weapons drawn and engaged.

"That could be him," Simon said from between clenched teeth. The tone he used left no doubt what he'd like to do to the man if he was on the other side of that door.

Blue moved forward, but Maverick held her back. "Take a position to the left of the door," he instructed quietly. He inclined his head toward Simon. "You step into the parlor there in case we need backup."

Both obeyed the older man without question or pause.

Maverick walked noiselessly to the door. He peered through the viewfinder, then drew back. He gestured for Blue to take a look.

She closed one eye and squinted through the small peephole, surveying the man who stood on the dimly lit porch. He wore a classic gray suit and wire-rimmed eyeglasses.

Edgar Rothman.

She recognized him from a photo she'd seen in Noah's profile. She'd completely forgotten that he was on his way. It was about time. It was a good thing Noah hadn't needed him after all.

"It's Rothman," she whispered to Maverick.

"You're sure it's him?" he whispered back.

She thought about that for a moment, recalling the group photo in the case file.

Rothman pounded on the door again.

"It's him. He's just late."

"All right."

Maverick jerked his head toward the left of the door. She resumed her position there. He rolled his head, stretching out his neck, then unlocked and opened the door in one swift, smooth motion.

"Where's—"

Before Rothman could complete his question, Maverick yanked him inside and shoved him against the door, closing it with the frightened scientist's body weight. "Turn around and spread 'em, buddy," he ordered.

Rothman adopted a look of disdain. "I beg your pardon?"

Maverick whirled him around, pressing his jaw against the polished wood, and quickly frisked him. He didn't care for the scientific type. Especially one that kept him waiting.

"This is an outrage!"

Blue almost laughed. This guy had to be on the up-

and-up. No self-respecting bad guy would make that kind of statement.

"Sorry, Mr. Rothman," Maverick said after checking his ID, and clearly not sorry at all. "Just had to be sure."

His glasses askew, Rothman turned around slowly and glared from one to the other. He quickly straightened his eyewear. "You don't know what a time I had getting here. And that truck I rented from some guy at that BullDog bar, well, let me tell you, the drive over was harrowing. The fellow who owned it claimed he was too far into the bottle to drive. Pitched me the keys for a mere twenty dollars." He glared at Maverick. "Are there any more indignities I should expect?" Not waiting for an answer, he turned his attention back to Blue. "How is Noah?"

"Much better," she assured him.

"I'd like to see him now, please." Rothman adjusted his jacket and shot another irritable look at Maverick. "I apologize for the delay. Flights were backed up for hours in D.C."

Blue didn't doubt that. Her own flight here had been delayed in addition to the annoying baggage checks. "He's not here right now, Mr. Rothman. But he'll be back any moment. He's with the rest of my team."

He looked taken aback, but rebounded swiftly enough. "I was under the impression he needed medical attention." He shook his head before Blue could answer as if the whole situation was more than he wanted to attempt comprehending. "I also want to try and persuade him to try the new antidote I've developed."

Blue's gaze riveted to his. "New antidote?"

He nodded. "If my conclusions are correct, as I'm

convinced they are, this will reverse all side effects related to the implant.''

Hope burgeoned in Blue's chest. If he could do that...

Noah would have his life back.

Chapter Fourteen

By four a.m., Logan, Ferrelli and Maverick had headed for the mainland. Max and Simon, her new Colby Agency friends, had said their goodbyes as well. Noah and Rothman were in the parlor going back and forth as to whether or not the antidote was worth the risk.

Chester had made a pot of strong coffee and was hanging out in the kitchen per Blue's request. She'd need a way to leave when the time came.

And that time was almost upon her.

The threat to Noah, apparently, had never existed. Leberman was nowhere to be found. Though the mouth of the cave where it opened onto the beach had been closed off by steel bars when Noah first discovered its existence, now there was a gate and a key. Leberman had uncovered Noah's secret and made himself a duplicate key, probably months ago. Mission Recovery and the Colby Agency planned to set up a special joint task force to try and run him down.

General Regan Bonner had apparently disappeared. No further intel had come in regarding any untoward activities on his part. There was nothing else here for Blue to do. Noah had to make it clear to Director

Casey that he required no protection. Blue strongly disagreed, but she couldn't force him to accept her help.

Victoria had called and given an update on Lucas, he was in stable condition. Casey had informed Logan that Ramon's condition had been upgraded to stable. Ramon had regained consciousness and there appeared to be no brain damage.

A locksmith would come to the island later in the day to install new locks on all the doors and windows in Noah's house. Casey had suggested a security company who could install an advanced system, which would be monitored and offered cutting-edge technology. But the man who wouldn't admit that he needed a bodyguard wasn't likely to own up to needing that kind of additional security.

Not even now, after all he'd been through.

Chester had agreed to take up the slack for Noah until he could hire a new assistant.

Noah apparently didn't need her in any capacity.

Hurt speared Blue's heart at the thought, but it was true. Why would he need her around? He could take care of himself. She'd seen that firsthand. Had the threat not come from within his own home, no one could have touched him.

Despite his debilitating condition, Noah was a strong man and quite capable of protecting himself as long as he wasn't exposed to bright light.

Even that might be about to change. Blue moved through the doorway into the parlor to see if the two had reached any sort of agreement.

"You're still only offering fifty-fifty odds, Edgar," Noah countered. "That's no better than what you offered before."

"There's a difference this time," Edgar argued. He paced behind the sofa facing Noah's position in the matching armchair. "True, I can only offer you a fifty-fifty chance the serum will work. However, this time the possibility of side effects is reduced to less than ten percent. You can try it without any real risk to speak of."

Sounded reasonable to Blue, but then she wasn't the one facing the ten-percent possibility that her brain's ability to function would be damaged by the new serum. Despite the hurt tearing her apart inside, her heart went out to Noah. She studied his handsome features, that chiseled face and those broad, strong shoulders. She would never forget how it felt to be held in those capable arms...or how skilled a lover he was. Instantly, her body reacted to the thought. She quickly focused her attention elsewhere. She would be leaving shortly. It was pointless to torture herself by considering what could have been or wishing things could be different. Noah Drake had been her assignment, falling for him wasn't anyone's fault but her own.

Noah looked straight at Blue then. "We have to talk—privately."

Edgar paused in his incessant pacing. "I'm certain I smell coffee brewing, perhaps I'll take a short break in the kitchen."

Noah nodded, clearly thankful for the reprieve. Edgar Rothman had no intention of taking no for an answer.

When he'd gone, Noah stood and moved toward her. Even the way he walked disrupted the rhythm of her heart. How would she ever get over this man?

"So, what do you think?" he asked, that dark gaze at once tender and penetrating.

She folded her arms over her chest to prevent herself from reaching out and touching him. She wanted so desperately to do just that. But leaving was going to be hard enough without the reminder of how her body responded to his. She had to remember that he wanted her to go. Their lives were so different, even she had to admit that.

"With the reduced risk, it's doable, I think." She hesitated, deeply appreciating his asking for her opinion, but at the same time afraid to be the one responsible for his trying what might prove detrimental to his well-being. "But, Noah," she searched those dark depths, aching to hold him and pretend nothing else mattered at the moment "this is a decision that you have to make on your own. It's your life."

She didn't add that she wanted desperately to share it with him…to be there every morning when he opened his eyes. How had she let that happen?

He nodded, the movement a barely discernible up-and-down motion. "I suppose you're impatient to be on your way. There's probably another mission waiting for you already."

She tried to read the flash of emotion in his eyes, but couldn't. Was it regret? Most likely not. She had no place in his world…just as her world left no margin for this kind of commitment.

She almost told him that she could take a few days off with Casey's blessing. The suggestion had been her director's, in fact. But that would sound like a plea to stay. She wouldn't do that. If Noah wanted her to stay, he would ask. Even then it would only be temporary…and make leaving all the more difficult.

"Yeah. I should be going. Chester's waiting." She

hitched a thumb toward the door. "I'll just go gather my things."

She turned away, praying he wouldn't notice the tears in her eyes. She didn't want him to see her cry. Dammit. It was bad enough she had to know it.

"Wait." He wrapped those long, strong fingers around her arm, staying her departure. "I want you to know how much—"

"You don't have to say anything, Noah." She cut off what would most likely be an attempt at thanks. A thank-you was not what she needed to hear. "It was my job."

She walked away, leaving him to think what he would. It would be better for both of them if they remembered that her being here had been a job... nothing more.

Maybe she could fool Noah, but nothing she said or did would fool her own heart.

NOAH WATCHED her go, knowing that the words she said were as far from the truth as could be. He'd heard the hurt in her voice...had seen the brightness of her eyes. She didn't want to go any more than he wanted her to, but it was the only way.

For now.

If there was any chance Edgar's new serum would work, Noah had to try. *If* he could get his life back there might just be hope for the two of them. Despite the risk involved, he would do this.

He would do it for her.

Noah went in search of Edgar. He might as well give him the news right away. The man teetered on the edge of outright hysteria. He seemed to want so desperately to right the wrong he felt solely responsible for.

After several minutes of discussion, Edgar announced that they should retire to the parlor for him to begin the treatment. He'd already set up a makeshift work area there shortly after arriving, according to Blue.

Noah only shook his head as he followed Edgar into the entry hall.

"I'm ready to go."

Noah turned at the sound of Blue's voice. She slowly descended the stairs, two duffel bags in tow. He met her at the foot of the staircase to relieve her of the bags, but Chester butted in.

"I'll take care of those, Mr. Drake," he insisted.

Noah relented since he'd rather spend his final moments with Blue without anything in the way.

She turned to Edgar and extended her hand. "Good bye, Mr. Rothman. I hope the serum works."

He shook her hand. "I'm certain it will."

She turned to Noah then, and his heart lurched. She offered her hand. "Take care, Noah. I wish you all the best."

He looked at her hand a moment, then reached past it and pulled her close. He kissed her hard on the mouth, forcing her to acknowledge what she wanted to deny...she wanted him still. They needed each other...wanted each other.

Her fingers fisted in his shirt and she kissed him back, confessing to all his heart already knew.

Then she pulled away and stared up at him, her lips trembling. "Good bye, Noah."

She followed Chester out the door without a backward glance.

Noah watched until the taillights of the old truck had disappeared from sight, then he closed and locked the door out of habit.

"Will she be back?" Edgar asked, standing only a few feet behind him.

Noah faced him, anger and pain exploding inside him. "Unless your serum works, I don't want her to come back. I would live the rest of my life alone before I would sentence her to this."

"Let's begin," Edgar suggested meekly.

Noah settled into a chair next to Edgar's prepared table. An IV pole stood behind the chair. Within a couple of minutes Edgar had inserted the IV needle into Noah's right arm and started the intravenous drip. The serum would be injected in two doses within five minutes of each other. Edgar had explained that it wasn't safe to inject it directly.

Noah closed his eyes and took a deep breath. *This is for you, Maggie Callahan.* He allowed snippets of the time they'd shared to flash quickly through the private theater of his mind and then he relaxed fully. "Let's do it," he said to Edgar, opening his eyes and settling his gaze on the other man's.

Edgar injected the first syringe full of serum via the intravenous line. Noah felt the burn as it entered his bloodstream. He tensed only for a moment, then forced himself to relax once more.

"How are you doing?" Edgar asked.

"Fine." Noah didn't look at him now. Instead, he allowed the minutes he and Blue had spent making love to replay over and over in his head. The burn disappeared, all else faded into nothing, as he relived those tender moments. No matter what happened, he would always have that.

The introduction of the second injection had little effect as far as Noah could tell. No burn...no dizziness...nothing. What he would label a distant headache had started in his skull. It wasn't disturbing just yet, but it was there, somewhere way in the back of his head.

"How do you feel now?" Edgar asked as he sat down directly in front of Noah.

Noah conducted a quick survey. "Nothing but a mild headache."

Edgar nodded. "That's to be expected considering what the serum is attempting to do."

As Noah understood it, the serum would actually pinpoint the implant and attempt to neutralize the cells there, effectively destroying their ability to function, thus leaving Noah in his former—as God intended— state. If that happened he and Blue could have a life together. If it didn't...

"How will we know if it worked?" Noah hadn't thought of that until now.

"We'll start by increasing the wattage of light in the room. We'll do it in slow increments so as not to cause any pain or damage if the serum has failed."

Noah nodded. Sounded reasonable. But time consuming.

"How long do we have to wait?"

"I'd like to give the serum a full twenty-four hours to do its work."

Rothman checked Noah's blood pressure again. "You're staying amazingly calm," he noted aloud.

"I want this to work." His gaze connected fully with Edgar's. "There are things I want to do."

Rothman sighed. "I imagine there are."

The telephone rang. The sound set Noah's nerves

on edge. He forced himself to calm. It was probably some of Blue's team wanting to know if she'd left yet.

He nodded to the phone and said to Edgar, "Do you mind?"

"Certainly not." Edgar picked up the cordless handset just as it rang a third time and brought it to Noah.

Noah depressed the Talk button. "Drake here."

He couldn't remember the last time he'd even answered a phone.

"Hello, Drake, hope you're doing well this morning."

Ice slid through Noah's veins.

General Regan Bonner.

"What do you want?" Noah demanded, his teeth clenched in rage. He could very well be on the verge of getting his life back. He didn't want this sick SOB interfering…not now that Noah actually had a reason to want it back.

"I want to make you pay for what you took from me," Bonner said as if Noah should have known the answer without asking. "Five years of my life. Not to mention my wife and daughter, neither of whom will even speak to me now."

"That was your own doing," Noah lashed out.

The bastard laughed. "I guess we'll just have to agree to disagree on that one. Now, let's get down to business. I'm at the cart-rental warehouse near the dock. You leave now and come straight here and we'll set this matter to rights."

Near the dock! Blue would be there about now, catching a ride from Mr. Venable. Chester had made the arrangements.

"No," Noah demanded. "You come here."

Another evil laugh. "I don't think so, Drake. This is my war, we'll fight it on my terms. Now, you have ten minutes to get here or I'll slit your girlfriend's throat. Or maybe I'll just poke out those pretty blue eyes and then slit her throat later."

Fear knotted in Noah's gut.

Too late.

He had Blue already.

"I'm on my way." Noah dropped the telephone and stood. He ripped off the tape holding the needle in his arm and removed it, wincing at the sting.

"What are you doing?" Edgar looked flustered. "Who was that on the phone?"

"Give me your keys."

"What?"

"You rented that old truck you arrived in from someone. It's still there. I saw it when I came back a couple hours ago. You must still have the keys."

Edgar reached into his pocket and removed the keys. "Tell me what's happened. Where is it you're going?"

Noah leveled a gaze on him that let him know there would be no more questions. "The general is here. He's got Blue."

He snatched the keys and headed for the front door.

"Wait!" Edgar shouted, running past him to get to the door first. "It's no more than twenty minutes or so until sunrise."

Noah reached for the lock and the doorknob simultaneously. "I don't have a choice."

Edgar stayed his hand when he would have opened the door. "What if—?"

"Step out of my way, Rothman."

Edgar blinked, the lethal tone Noah had used getting

through. He nodded, then stepped aside. "I've done all I can."

Noah looked at him one last time before leaving. The man was behaving even more bizarrely than normal. "Call Director Casey. See if he can get some of his people back here. Hell, call the sheriff. Chester's probably hurt out there, if not dead. They're holding her at the rental warehouse. Blue will need the backup in case Bonner..."

He didn't have to say the rest.

NOAH DROVE to Weber's general store and parked the truck. He'd passed Chester's vehicle en route. The man was wounded but alive. Noah suffered a moment of vertigo now as he climbed out. The damned serum was starting to play havoc with his senses. He could see and hear normally, but he suffered a number of visual disturbances. Depth perception and the like.

The sun hovered just beneath the horizon. Already pink and gold hues were streaking across the sky. He had to hurry. As quickly as he dared, he moved toward the warehouse. Once he'd found a suitable route of entrance, he concentrated hard to invoke the chameleon process.

Within five seconds his exposed flesh was as dark as the night. He knew a moment of regret. Well, at least he didn't have to wonder or harbor false hope. Edgar's serum had failed to even slow down the process. At the moment, rescuing Blue was all that mattered. Noah had never really held out hope that his condition could be changed. Forcing all other thought from his mind, he entered the building.

"BEFORE DRAKE DIES, I want him to watch you die a slow, painful death," the general said to Blue.

He leaned down, putting his face close to hers. "Perhaps then we'll be *almost* even. But I won't rest until the sun rises and destroys him once and for all."

She spat in the man's face and told him what he could do as far as she was concerned.

He slapped her so hard she barely remained conscious. Stars appeared behind her closed lids. At least she'd had her say. Five of his cohorts were standing by, anticipating Noah's arrival. There could be more, but she'd only counted five. She had to stay alert so that she could attempt to help Noah when he arrived. She'd worked until the ropes binding her hands were somewhat looser. The skin was rubbed raw at her wrists, it stung like hell but the blood would facilitate her ability to slip free. Except she had to be careful that no one noticed what she was up to.

The light in the warehouse was not bright by any means, but it was stronger than the watts Noah could take, she was sure. She didn't want to think what kind of pain Noah would endure just coming inside. And then, if they survived, he would not be able to leave since the sun would be up. What was she saying? Rothman's serum could be killing him already. He'd said only a ten-percent risk of harmful side effects, but he could be wrong. If only she could break free and escape before Noah arrived…or in time to help him if he needed her. A part of her hoped he didn't come.

She might still escape without any assistance.

Surely Rothman would know what to do if things took a turn for the worse with the serum.

One of the general's men grunted and suddenly crumpled to the floor.

All eyes turned in that direction.

Nothing. No one was there.

Noah was here.

Blue struggled harder to free her hands. Though she was unarmed, she could fight.

Another guard dropped.

All hell broke loose then.

The remaining men scrambled to fight what they couldn't see. The general shouted orders.

Then the unexpected happened. Noah was suddenly standing right in front of the general for all to see.

He held the .38 Blue had left behind aimed right at the general's forehead. "Tell them to let her go," Noah commanded, his tone soft but unmistakably dangerous.

Tears welled in Blue's eyes at the sight of him. Her heart hurtled into double-time. He'd come for her. But it would surely cost him his life.

She jerked hard against her bindings.

"Go ahead," the general said, laughing, "kill me. My men have orders to kill her first and then you. They won't hesitate even if I'm dead. You see, that's what I've waited for all this time. It wasn't enough that you were sentenced to darkness. I wanted more."

Blue was almost free. If only he kept talking…

"I've had people watching you from the beginning. I could have taken you out one month ago or two years ago. You certainly didn't appear to care. But I waited. I wanted you to suffer just as I had. I needed to be patient until you developed an attachment. The right kind of attachment." His smile was menacing, cruel. "I must say that I've enjoyed watching the goose chase your man Lowell took you on. But, more important, this moment has been worth the wait. She's going to die and you're going to be the reason. For a very, very short time you'll live with that reality. Then we'll be even.''

Pain etched deeply across his face, Noah drew the hammer back with a resounding *click* of metal on metal. ''But you won't see any of it.''

''I'll die relishing the triumph,'' the general returned.

Suddenly Blue was free.

The attention of the three remaining guards was focused on Noah and the general. She had to make a move…distract them.

She slung the closest object, a bicycle chain, to the right and dashed between the carts and bicycles to her left.

Gunfire erupted.

Unfortunately, the guards weren't the only ones distracted.

Concerned for her welfare, Noah took his eyes off the general for a split second. The general knocked him to the floor. The .38 discharged when it hit, then slid several feet on the concrete. Blue made a dive for it, then rolled to cover.

She got off a single shot, disabling one of the guards. Then she fired again, knocking out the main overhead light. The room dimmed considerably.

Noah gained the upper hand on the general.

Darting through the maze of carts, Blue moved into a better position to bring down yet another guard.

Only one left.

The general regained control.

Blue tried not to focus on that. She needed…

''Drop it.''

The last guard was right behind her.

A weapon exploded. Once…twice. The second bullet whizzed just over her head. The guard dropped.

Noah staggered to his feet, the general's weapon in his hands.

The general lay crumpled on the floor.

Blue scrambled from her hiding place and hurried to Noah. He looked ready to drop himself.

"We have to get you out of this light." She ushered him toward the darker side of the building. The fluorescent lights were high overhead directly in the middle of the warehouse. Though she'd put the main one out of commission, the wattage was still too much. The outer perimeter of the warehouse was blessedly dimmer.

"You okay?" Noah's voice was tight, laced with the pain he could not hide. But his only concern was for her, she could see that. Her heart melted with an emotion that scared her to death.

"Don't try to talk. Rest. There has to be a phone in here. I'll call Rothman." She didn't like the way Noah looked. Pale, lifeless. The serum. Was this a reaction to the serum or to the light?

A grating, rattling sound echoed from the front of the warehouse.

She needed to find out the source of the noise but Noah's eyes had closed and he'd leaned back against the nearest crate sending a new flood of worry through her.

"Noah." She shook him gently.

Light spilled across the concrete. The screech of metal hissed through the air.

Fear sped through her veins as, seemingly in slow motion, her head turned toward the light.

Someone was opening the large overhead door.

The sun was up. Light filled the warehouse, crowding out the darkness.

Blue tried to shield Noah with her body. The semiautomatic weapon belonging to the general slipped from his limp fingers. She reached for it, her gaze never leaving the silhouetted figure standing in the now fully open doorway.

She started to raise the weapon…

"Put it down. *Now.*"

Disbelief held her in suspended animation for two beats.

The figure stepped forward, his own weapon leveled on her.

Edgar Rothman.

She tightened her grip on the gun and took a bead. "Close that door or I'll shoot."

Rothman laughed. "No you won't. Because I'll shoot Noah. You might kill me, but I'll kill him."

He was right. His aim was now directed at Noah. He might be a scientist, but who knew what kind of marksman he was.

Noah groaned.

"You're killing him!" she cried, her hands beginning to tremble in spite of her best efforts. Why was Rothman doing this? Reality jolted her like a lightening strike. He was the mole…the man on the inside. The one who'd helped Leberman.

"Precisely," Rothman said. "Even if you stopped me now, which is highly unlikely, that slow-working poison I injected will kill him within a few hours."

Blue shook her head. "Why?"

Rothman smiled. "For the money. What else? Leberman made me an offer I couldn't refuse. It's a shame the general and his men didn't take care of the two of you and save me the trouble. Although I must admit that Bonner's sudden appearance was unexpected, I'm disappointed he failed. Be that as it may, as soon as the two of you are dead, I'm rushing to the hospital where Lucas and Victoria are. I won't have any trouble getting in, especially when I tell them that Leberman has struck again. Then I'll finish Lucas and retire in style." He adopted a look of annoyance. "If Leberman had done his part, I wouldn't be in this position. I wasn't supposed to have to kill anyone. But, you see, he had to leave in a hurry. So, unfortunately, it's my job to finish what he started, one way or another. That was the deal. Once you're all dead, I get the rest of my money."

She shook her head again. "You were supposed to be Director Casey's friend…Noah's friend. I can't believe this."

"You don't have to. You're dead."

Rothman swung his aim in her direction.

Two shots echoed in rapid succession.

Blue stumbled back.

She was hit.

But only once…she thought.

There had been two shots.

She hadn't discharged her weapon…

Noah. Was he hit? The poison…

The lights suddenly dimmed.

She swayed. Her knees buckled.

The concrete floor flew up to meet her. It felt cold beneath her.

Chapter Fifteen

Three Months Later

Finally, an assignment.

Blue took a seat in front of Lucas's desk at Mission Recovery's headquarters and tried to contain her anticipation. The secretary had said that he would be right back and that Blue should wait. She had been on light duty for three long months. After what felt like an eternity jockeying a desk, the doctor had allowed her to return to field duty.

She forced away the thoughts of Noah that immediately resurrected. She couldn't think about him. It still hurt too much. All she had left of him was that painting and she stared at it for hours on end each night. How pathetic was that?

Edgar Rothman had almost succeeded in killing him. But somehow Noah had survived.

Blue still couldn't come to terms with Rothman's duplicity. The man had claimed to be Noah's friend as well as Director Casey's. And he'd tried to destroy them both, Noah personally and Casey professionally. Lucas had explained to her that Rothman's failure with the chameleon implant had pushed him over the edge.

At one time he had been a brilliant research scientist, a genius. The failure and subsequent downgrade in his position with the government had turned him bitter and angry. But no one had suspected. He showed up for work every day and pretended all was well.

His bitterness had only deepened as Thomas Casey had continued to move up the ranks. The idea that Casey was successful and he was not had, apparently, been too much to take. In the end, Rothman had seen Noah as part of the reason his life and career were a failure. Transference of guilt was not uncommon in this kind of case. At least that's what the shrinks said. Blue had always heard that genius was only a narrow margin away from insanity. Rothman had proven that when he accepted Leberman's offer. Of course the money had been substantial. From what they'd discovered among Rothman's bank accounts and other personal belongings, Leberman had already provided him with more money than he could hope to make in several lifetimes as a researcher.

And then there was Leberman…still at large.

Thoughts of Noah managed to trickle into her musings. He'd saved her life by managing to get off that one shot, killing Rothman. But Rothman had put a bullet in her, a little too high to be lethal, but it had screwed up her shoulder pretty badly. Still, she was thankful Rothman had turned out to be a lousy shot. And even more thankful Noah hadn't allowed him a second attempt to improve his standing.

Busy cleaning up, the owner from BullDog's bar had called the sheriff after hearing the gunfire. When he'd realized it was safe to approach the building, he'd closed the overhead door for Noah. Then the guy had stayed with Noah and Blue, though she had no recall of it, until help arrived. And Lucas had thought the islanders weren't friendly.

In the hospital, after surgery, Blue had learned that Noah had been taken into custody by the organization where Rothman had worked...where Noah had once worked.

Though she'd tried to contact him several times that first month after leaving the hospital, she'd had no luck. Finally, she'd given up. Well, actually, Lucas had ordered her to stop trying. He would only tell her that Noah was alive and receiving treatment.

She was grateful that he was alive.

"Sorry to keep you waiting, Callahan," Lucas said as he came in and settled into the leather executive's chair behind his wide mahogany desk.

"No problem, sir." She pushed all other thoughts from her mind and focused on the man before her. Lucas was fully recovered as well. He appeared to have suffered no permanent complications.

He folded his hands atop the blotter on his desk and settled that penetrating gray gaze on hers. "I'm afraid this meeting is not about a new assignment. In fact, I'd like you to take a couple of weeks of actual vacation starting now."

"What?" Shock, quickly followed by ire, quaked through her. "I'm ready for an assignment. I've been on desk duty for—"

Lucas held up a hand silencing her. "This is a direct order from Casey."

Blue seethed. This was ridiculous, that's what it was. Casey would hear about this.

Lucas picked up a small envelope. "I think this will explain the reasoning behind our decision." He passed the envelope to Blue.

Trying her best to contain her fury, she ripped the envelope open and pulled out what looked like an invitation. The embossed front depicted a local Georgetown art gallery. Recognition flared. It was the gallery where she'd purchased Noah's painting. Her fingers suddenly cold and trembling, she opened the invitation and stared at the printed words inside.

The Nelson Gallery cordially invites you to the premiere showing of the works of Noah David Drake on Friday, October 27, at 5:00 p.m.

Her heart thundered into a run. That was today.

Her gaze locked with Lucas's. "What's this about?"

His expression gave nothing away. "That is the first of many showings and personal appearances to come if the critics are right about his work."

She shook her head. "No, I mean is he all right? Really all right?"

Lucas nodded. "There was no antidote. Rothman lied. Nearly a year ago, however, one of his protégés came up with a surgical procedure to *fix* things, but Rothman never mentioned it to Noah since that's about the time Leberman approached him."

She could scarcely breathe. "So he's okay? The light…"

"The condition is completely stabilized. No side effects whatsoever. But it was a painful process. A dangerous process. Nothing like Rothman had suggested. Noah didn't want you to know. He had to undergo extensive surgery and then weeks of rehabilitation."

Blue blinked furiously to hold back the gathering

tears. "So, he's okay and he wants to see me?" She looked at the invitation. "This was his idea?"

Lucas smiled. "Yes on all counts. That's why we knew you'd need a couple of weeks off. Drake said something about a long, private, secluded vacation on some mountain in Switzerland."

Blue stood, almost dizzy with happiness. "I...I have to go." She had to find just the right dress. She had to...

What she felt certain was an absolutely moonstruck smile slid across her lips. Noah wanted to be with her. They could have a life together now. "I have to go," she repeated.

"See you in two weeks, Callahan," Lucas said as she rushed out of his office.

She tossed him a wave without slowing down. It was three already. She had to hurry.

Blue grabbed her purse from her desk and took the stairs two at a time. She was too keyed up to wait for the elevator. Noah was waiting for her.

BLUE HESITATED outside the Nelson Gallery. She considered the little black dress and spiked heels she wore. Noah had never seen her dressed like this and with her hair fashioned in a French twist. What if he didn't like it? What if the two weeks in Switzerland was all he wanted?

She couldn't keep torturing herself.

Fortifying herself with a deep breath, she entered the elegant, quiet gallery. She was early, few patrons had arrived as yet. The climate-controlled air made her shiver. She smiled, her pulse leaping. Or maybe it was the man waiting for her just inside the door.

"Hello, Blue."

The black tailored suit was one of the narrow fitting designer ones. The crisp white shirt was open at the throat and displayed a few inches of that magnificent chest. She swallowed tightly. He looked wonderful. His thick, dark hair was a little shorter, but otherwise...perfect.

"Hello, Noah."

They stared at each other for a very long time. Both content simply to look.

Her heart was pounding so hard in her chest that she could scarcely draw a breath, but she couldn't take her eyes off him. He was really here. It was still daylight outside and he was free of the curse that had plagued him for five long years.

He had his life back.

"I've missed you," he said finally in that dark, enigmatic voice.

"I've missed you," she echoed.

He looked away for a moment. Her heart lurched. Was this the part where he let her down easy? No, she wouldn't accept that.

His gaze collided with hers once more. "I was thinking that we should spend some time together, alone, getting to know each other. *Really* getting to know each other."

She clenched her fingers around the tiny black beaded bag in her hand. "I have some time off coming." She hardly recognized her voice. She sounded so uncertain...so small.

He moved a step closer. "I've thought of nothing but you for three months," he said softly. "You were all that got me through the pain of recovery."

She blinked at the tears welling. "I wanted to see you."

He shook his head slowly as he moved yet another step nearer. "I needed to be whole before I saw you again. I needed to be sure I could offer you what you deserved."

"Noah—"

He raised a hand, cutting off her protest. "I want you in my life *permanently*. I want us to restore the house together in our spare time. I want us to walk the beach in the moonlight…to have children…to just be…together."

She was the one who moved this time, taking a tiny step forward…toward that fairy-tale life he'd just painted with all the right words. "I'd like that very much."

Finally, just when she thought she'd die if one more second passed, he took her into his arms and kissed her. She knew without doubt that she would spend the rest of her life loving this man. Like finding that painting of his…it was fate.

LUCAS SAT at a table in an open-air coffee shop and watched Blue enter the Nelson Gallery only a few yards away, across the small cobblestone plaza. The moment she entered the ritzy joint, Noah Drake approached her. They talked for a while, then he took her into his arms. The kiss went on and on.

"Do you think they'll come up for air anytime soon?"

Lucas turned his attention across the table to Thomas Casey. "Probably not."

Casey shook his head. "To be that young and in love." His expression turned serious then. "Do you think we're going to lose one of our best Specialists? Drake did tell you he intended to make her his wife."

Lucas shifted his attention to the couple going for a record-breaking kiss in the gallery window. A few passersby had stopped to watch the show.

"No, I don't think we'll lose her," Lucas said with complete certainty. "I think we're going to gain a hell of an intelligence officer to add to our ranks. One who has a real *gift*."

Casey nodded. "We could use Drake."

Lucas's smile widened. "But first we'll have to wait until they've made up for lost time." Lucas scooted back from the table, preparing to go. He'd only come to see the reunion. Not that he was a romantic or anything...but he was a sucker for happy endings. He thought of Victoria and wondered if they would ever have a chance at a happy ending. "Well, I have work to do."

"One more thing," Casey said, waylaying him.

Lucas knew that tone, that look. Casey was worried about something. "What's up?"

"I don't think we're going to find Leberman until he makes another move to do harm to either you or Victoria."

Lucas shrugged casually but his gut clenched with pure hatred. "I agree. He's too smart to be caught so easily. He's stayed underground for years at a time before. I don't expect any less this time. He'll keep us waiting, anticipating, until he thinks we've let down our guard. Then he'll start his game again."

"You still haven't told me everything," Casey prodded knowingly.

Lucas exhaled a heavy breath. "James Colby and Errol Leberman were in military intelligence together. There was a terrible tragedy. Leberman lost his entire family. He lost it and somehow got the idea that James was responsible. He swore he'd have his revenge.'' Lucas shook his head. "He killed James. I can't prove it, but I know it. Leberman is determined to destroy all that belonged to James.''

"We'll stop him,'' Casey offered reassuringly.

"Victoria has suffered enough,'' Lucas added wearily. "She lost her husband and her son.''

"Did Leberman have anything to do with the son?''

"I believe he did, but there's no proof.'' Lucas made a sound of disgust. "What makes it so bad is the fact that Leberman and I have had the same training. He knows all the tricks. He won't be easy to stop.''

Casey's gaze locked with Lucas's. "So we wait?''

Lucas knew it was a more or less rhetorical question, but he responded just the same. "We wait. And this time when he rears that ugly head out of whatever hole he's hiding in, I'm going to finish this once and for all.''

Casey had no doubt that he would. Lucas Camp was a man of his word. Casey still felt guilty that he'd allowed Lucas to go to that island in his stead, but then, Leberman had counted on Lucas doing just that.

Casey watched as Lucas strode slowly toward the car waiting to take him back to Mission Recovery. Casey was in no hurry. He turned back to the gallery just across the small plaza. Lucas was right about that too. There was nothing like a happy ending.

* * * *

If you enjoyed THE SPECIALISTS *then look out for another story in Debra Webb's exciting* THE COLBY AGENCY *series—Her Secret Alibi—on the shelves in June 2004.*

SILHOUETTE®
INTRIGUE™

AVAILABLE FROM 16TH JANUARY 2004

DADDY TO THE RESCUE Susan Kearney

Heroes Inc.

Ex-marine Kirk Hardaker had to rescue ex-wife Sara from a plane crash in the mountains. But a killer was intent on destroying Sara and her child to get her top secret computer software. Could Kirk reach them before the killer struck and protect the family he'd always wanted?

PHANTOM LOVER Rebecca York

43 Light Street

In the darkened bedroom of Ravencrest mansion PI Bree Brennan was seduced by an unseen lover. A lover whose scorching kiss was strangely familiar. Was her midnight caller Troy London, her one-time love—a man who'd disappeared and she'd been sent to find?

FAKE ID WIFE Patricia Rosemoor

Club Undercover

Desperate mother on the run Elise Mitchell never imagined that posing as the wife of sexy Logan Smith would be her only hope of saving her child from the clutches of a killer. But when she accepted the protection of his name, it was hard to fight the forever feeling of their for-now vows.

UNDER LOCK AND KEY Sylvie Kurtz

When Tyler Blackwell awoke from a minor car crash to find himself under lock and key in a castle dungeon, he found that being Melissa's 'prisoner' had its advantages. Could Tyler penetrate the wall of stone surrounding Melissa's heart and gain her trust before a killer struck?

proudly presents

a new batch of stories from

Julie Miller

The Taylor Clan

*One family of strong, honourable men
—sworn to uphold the law.*

SUDDEN ENGAGEMENT

January 2004

IN THE BLINK OF AN EYE

March 2004

THE ROOKIE

May 2004

KANSAS CITY'S BRAVEST

July 2004

0104/SH/LC80

▼ SILHOUETTE®

turning
point

SHARON
SALA

Paula Detmer Riggs

Peggy Moreland

Three mysterious bouquets of red roses lead to three brand-new romances

On sale 16th January 2004

*Available at most branches of WH Smith,
Tesco, Martins, Borders, Eason, Sainsbury's
and all good paperback bookshops.*

0204/055/SH67

NORA ROBERTS

Table for Two

No.1 *New York Times* bestselling author

Summer Desserts *&* Lessons Learned

Available from 16th January 2004

*Available at most branches of WHSmith,
Tesco, Martins, Borders, Eason, Sainsbury's
and most good paperback bookshops.*

SILHOUETTE®
DESIRE™

are proud to introduce

DYNASTIES:
THE BARONES

*Meet the wealthy Barones—caught in a
web of danger, deceit and…desire!*

Twelve exciting stories in six 2-in-1 volumes:

2 FREE

books and a surprise gift!

We would like to take this opportunity to thank you for reading this Silhouette® book by offering you the chance to take TWO more specially selected titles from the Intrigue™ series absolutely FREE! We're also making this offer to introduce you to the benefits of the Reader Service™—

★ FREE home delivery
★ FREE gifts and competitions
★ FREE monthly Newsletter
★ Exclusive Reader Service offers
★ Books available before they're in the shops

Accepting these FREE books and gift places you under no obligation to buy, you may cancel at any time, even after receiving your free shipment. Simply complete your details below and return the entire page to the address below. *You don't even need a stamp!*

YES! Please send me 2 free Intrigue books and a surprise gift. I understand that unless you hear from me, I will receive 4 superb new titles every month for just £2.90 each, postage and packing free. I am under no obligation to purchase any books and may cancel my subscription at any time. The free books and gift will be mine to keep in any case.

I4ZED

Ms/Mrs/Miss/Mr ....Initials....................................
                                                                                    BLOCK CAPITALS PLEASE
Surname ....
Address ....

....

....Postcode....................................

Send this whole page to:
UK: FREEPOST CN81, Croydon, CR9 3WZ
EIRE: PO Box 4546, Kilcock, County Kildare (stamp required)